THE FORGOTTEN TOMB OF THE KNIGHTS TEMPLAR

THE TEMPLAR LEGACY - BOOK 2

PRESTON WILLIAM CHILD

Edited by

ANGELA WALKER & JAMES BARNETT

PROLOGUE

THE SKEWERED

The battlefield had been dyed red with blood. Most of the freshly slain corpses were not on the ground but instead propped up by the enormous wooden stakes that were impaled through their bodies. It was unlike most mass graves in the world and was a display that those who witnessed would not soon forget. That was the point of it, at least. That was what most people believed—the skewered bodies were meant to be a barbaric warning to future enemies. It wasn't only the enemies that were terrified of the tactic, though. Some of the allies were just as afraid of it. That was mainly because they were afraid of their ruler and the one that had stuck those stakes through their defeated foes. After all, their leader was renowned for this tactic—the infamous Vlad the Impaler.

Andrei served in Vlad's army and helped impale those enemies to help perpetuate Vlad's favorite form of execution. It was never an easy task to complete, but no one dared to fail for fear that they would be the next ones that had an enormous spear of wood driven through them and that their last breaths would be spent suspended off of the ground and run through by one of those wooden stakes. Andrei was no different. He was a smart and capable warrior that was well aware of the cruelty that his leader often showed.

It was easy to serve someone that powerful, someone that inspired fear and loyalty in equal measure. There was a certain security to being on the side of that kind of a person, to know that most people would not dare try to harm you when they may have to face the Impaler's wrath if they tried anything. There were all sorts of stories about him, and no one knew what exactly was true and what was not, and no one dared to get too close to Vlad to ask.

Some said that Vlad the Impaler was not a mortal man but some kind of demonic beast. They could not believe that a human being would favor the kinds of methods that Vlad used, like skewering his enemies when he had already crushed them. The thing that had earned him his moniker was also what caused so many slanderous stories to be spread about him. No matter what the actual truth was, people were all just worried that they would someday end up as one of the people impaled.

It didn't matter to Andrei. It was not his job to try to understand Vlad. It was his job to follow his orders and serve him well as part of his military. So he did. He fought for Vlad, and when the fighting was done, he ran people through with that wooden stake. He was a dutiful soldier that never questioned his orders and never questioned Vlad's methods. A legendary man like that must have had good reason to be so cruel toward his enemies.

"Help...help me. Please...help. Please help me."

The voice came from behind Andrei, and just as he heard it, a drop of blood splashed down onto his forehead, running down the side of his face. He wiped it away once he saw what it was and turned around to find the source of the droplet. An impaled man was looming over his head, being propped up by one of those long wooden pikes. It had pierced his right shoulder, and now he was just wounded and slowly dying, with no chance of escaping or ever getting down. Soon that man would be like the rest of the skewered people around them, just another victim of Vlad the Impaler's methods.

"Please help me," the man begged weakly, lines of his insides spewing out of his mouth. "Please, you have to help me."

"I do not have to do anything," Andrei said coldly, just speaking the truth. "You may not have noticed, but you are not exactly in a position to make any demands. Look at you. You have lost, and you will never get down from there. You might as well just let yourself finish dying at this point. That would be the quickest way to make the pain stop."

The impaled man couldn't seem to hear him very well, probably already fading away from the mortal world. He stared at the ground at Andrei's feet and then choked on more blood that fell down off of his chin, nearly splashing Andrei.

"I am sure you fought well," Andrei said. "You have nothing to be ashamed of."

The wounded man ignored him again and spoke through his gurgling of blood, "I saw him."

"Saw who?"

"The Impaler. Your leader."

"That is not possible."

"Yes...yes, it is...I-I-I saw it with my...with my own two eyes. He was here on the battlefield. I have never...I have never seen a man ever m-mo-move like that in my entire life. It was...it was awful...that man is no man at all. No...no, Vlad the Impaler is a beast, a monster that should not exist in this world."

Andrei was well aware of all of those rumors about Vlad, but none of them phased him because all of those things came from people that barely knew the man. He was much closer to the truth than any of those people that just spread baseless conjecture about other people.

The impaled man choked on more and more blood. He should probably have been conserving whatever strength he had left instead of trying to convert Andrei to his line of thinking. Those were wastes of breath when he needed as much time as possible.

"You must believe me."

"I am afraid that I do not," Andrei said bluntly. "And even if there was truth to it, it has nothing to do with you. Not anymore."

"Then you will be the one to suffer him. We all will. The Impaler will drown this world with blood, and then he will devour all of the red oceans. You wait. You will see that I'm...you will see what I see...perhaps you will finally realize it when...when you are up here like me...when you have been run through by a wooden stake. He is a demon...and all he wants is blood."

Andrei watched the man die, but his words haunted him for years to come. He watched as Wallachia fell under more and more of a shadow as their leader showed his true colors. Slowly, Andrei started to believe the story of that impaled dead man. Vlad was not like the rest of the leaders in the world. He had another kind of power that none of the rest of them possessed and an insatiable lust for blood that even his greatest conquests did not seem able to satiate. Before long, Andrei started to not even think of the man as a human being anymore. He was a dark force of nature—the monster that their enemies proclaimed him to be. But it was that realization that cost him his life.

It was one night that he was summoned by their great leader when most of the rest of Wallachia was sleeping. Andrei stepped into Vlad's private chambers to tend to whatever his king needed. As Vlad stood in the shadows, he only had one request. He requested a drink—but unfortunately, he did not want it to be from a chalice. He wanted his drink to come from Andrei's throat.

The last thing Andrei remembered in his life was his king

enveloping him from the darkness and the feeling of blood running down his neck. Before long, his life was over, and he couldn't help but believe in all of those morbid tales about Vlad the Impaler then.

1

THE NEW STUDENT OF THE OCCULT

Jean-Luc Gerard still was not sure about the idea of teaching someone about actual magic, yet he was apparently doing it anyway. He had gotten quite used to spending his time alone in his occult bookshop, but now he was rarely ever alone there. His new apprentice was always rummaging through the shelves and asking ridiculous questions.

"Couldn't we do something to make this book just come straight to my hand or something? That would just be so much easier. There has got to be some kind of magic word for that, right?"

Thaddeus Rose was not the ideal student to have. As a self-proclaimed clairvoyant, necromancer and warlock when he was really just a fairly average street magician, he had too big of an ego to really take learning seriously. He couldn't really focus and always seemed to think that he knew best—or at least knew better than Jean. It was just ironic because he had been the one to come to Jean for lessons after seeing Jean perform real magic.

But the more he taught Thad, the clearer it was that it wasn't going to be easy. It didn't help that Jean was not really the teaching type. If he wanted to share information with someone, he usually would just lend them a book and let its contents do all of the actual teaching. But that wasn't exactly a possible strategy when it came to his new student since Thad seemed to have trouble focusing while reading.

"No, with real magic, there are no shortcuts. There are no tricks to get it done, and it's not just about misdirection like the so-called magic that you are used to."

Thad had gotten accustomed to his street magic and still thought of magic in those terms, no matter how hard Jean tried to change his perspective. He saw magic as a tool to be used in some kind of performance, as a means to awe and amaze people. With how far up his own ass he was, it was a difficult talk to try to shift a narcissist's point of view. Thad asking for Jean's help and showing real interest in magic must have been a brief moment of clarity in the sea of egomania that was Thaddeus Rose's brain.

"But really, though." Thad plopped a tall stack of old books on the table. "How many more of these things am I going to have to read?"

"As many as it takes," Jean said honestly. "And we have not even gotten to the best ones yet. Just wait until we get to the old scripts and scrolls where everything is in a dead language, so you have to decipher each and every word with different codexes. We haven't even touched those yet."

Thad did not look thrilled and especially didn't look excited. He brushed his purple streak of hair out of his face and scoffed, looking back to the book in front of him. He really looked lost and pathetic as he stared into an open book.

Jean still was not even sure why he was helping the street magician to begin with and why he was humoring this notion of Thaddeus Rose learning about actual magic. They weren't friends, and the only thing they had in common was their recent trip to the Winchester Mystery House. In that haunted mansion, Thad just showed Jean that he was an egotistical, self-centered, and incompetent idiot that cared more about looking for his social media posts than he cared about anything else. But on that trip, he had seen Jean use real magic and, since then, had looked at Jean with the kind of awe and respect that he didn't look at most people with. So when he showed up after they got back, asking to learn about actual magic instead of relying on his magician tricks, something compelled Jean to agree to teach him. It was probably pity, but he should have known that Thad would still be the same smug young man, no matter what he was doing. In order to be able to learn about something properly, a person needed to accept that they did not already know everything, and that was very hard for someone like Thad.

Thad was also challenging as a student because he was so easily distracted. Any stray thought he had could so easily turn into a whole rant that had nothing to do with what he was studying. Any sort of external stimulant would pull his attention away from his reading, too, no matter how small of a distraction it should have been. A bug flying on the other side of the room or a spider crawling up a wall would suddenly become the most fascinating thing in the world if it meant that he didn't have to keep reading. He was like a child or rebellious teenager that would do anything to try not to have to go to school.

It was starting to get a little bit frustrating, and Jean was already annoyed with Thaddeus Rose to begin with.

"You want to learn about magic, right? That's why you came here."

Thad looked up from the book that he was pretending to read. He looked like a kid that had been caught with his hand in a cookie jar.

"Yes, of course I do."

"Then you need to put in the time and, more importantly, the effort." Jean decided to just be brutally honest with his new apprentice. "Magic, the real kind of magic and not the stuff that you are used to showing people, can be extremely dangerous. It is a lot of power for one person to be able to harness. One wrong word and you can cause something disastrous to happen. You could fracture nature itself if you are not careful. It is for that reason that it is vital for someone to know what they are doing. This part, all of the studying and reading, may seem boring, but it is actually the most crucial part of it all. You need to sharpen your mind before you will ever come close to learning any actual spells or other parts of witchcraft. There is no room for error. So stop letting yourself get distracted, stop procrastinating, and get to work. Otherwise, this will all be a complete waste of time for you and for me."

Thaddeus looked like he had just been punched in the gut, and the reality of the situation, thankfully, seemed to dawn on him a little bit. He didn't try to make some pithy response or act like he was above it all, and instead, he didn't say a word. He just gave a few nods and then put his nose back in the book. He actually seemed to put all of his attention into what he was reading, which was exactly what he needed to do. Maybe a student like Thad just needed a firmer hand guiding him to new knowledge. Some people were like that. Hopefully that would do the trick, or Jean would end these lessons.

While Thad finally got to studying, Jean started sorting some of the books on the shelves in his shop. He had gotten a few new items that he had high hopes for, but he always read through them to make sure that they fit the standards of his store. Jean's bookstore was regarded well for not having any tacky items on its shelves, and he made sure to only have the most legitimate texts that dealt with the supernatural and the paranormal. His place of business held those topics in high regard and reflected how he felt about the topics too. His customer base appreciated that, and he did not like to let them down. That was what made all of those books good tools for someone like Thad to learn from, too, since he was only diving into magical lore that had at least some basis in fact. They wouldn't teach him about flying broomsticks or anything like that, at least.

Jean was surprised that Thaddeus spent the next couple of hours fully attentive to the books that he had been given. That conversation seemed to have gotten to him. It was nice to see him actually focused on something.

As Jean closed up the store, he interrupted Thad's focus and decided to reward him for the hard work he had done that evening.

"Hey, you up for getting a drink or something? Maybe some food? My treat."

Thaddeus Rose was not the kind of person that would turn down anything free. He slammed the book he was reading shut and practically leaped out of his chair. "Absolutely!"

The two of them walked through the streets of the French Quarter, which were brimming with people as always. The nightlife of New Orleans was always thrilling and energetic. All of the musicians filled the city with their music, so they helped bring the whole place to life. There was nothing quite like it and just being out and about in the city brought Jean so much joy. There was an undeniable magic to a place like that—and that was not even taking into account all of the magical culture and history of New Orleans. It was a hub for the mystical, the supernatural, the paranormal, and the unexplained.

They took a seat at a table outside of a bar and ordered drinks. There was a time when Jean would not have been caught dead socializing with Thaddeus Rose. It would be too damaging to his reputation for anyone to see him spending time with that fraud of a street magician. While it still was not ideal, it was better than it used to be because at least now it was just a mentor and an apprentice sharing a drink together after a hard day's work. It at least felt earned, and he didn't quite hate Thaddeus as much as he used to, even if the young man still annoyed him sometimes.

"So, what do Danielle and Kaleb think about your magic lessons?" Jean asked out of genuine curiosity.

Dani and Kaleb were part of Thad's crew for his street performances. Kaleb documented a lot of it, including pictures and videos for Thad's social media, while Dani was his handler and tried to help him boost his popularity. They were also some of his best friends, and Jean found them much more tolerable than the big star himself. He had actually gotten to know them quite well during all of that chaos at the Winchester Mystery House. Secretly, he kind of wished one of them had wanted to learn instead of Thaddeus. They were much more tolerable—a pleasure to be around, actually.

"They seem pretty happy about it. Plus, it means they don't have to put up with me as much as they used to."

That probably was a big blessing, and Jean was glad to be giving those two a reprieve from Thad's ego.

"They saw what you did back at the haunted house too, you know? So they know that I'm not just getting reeled into some scam. They know that I might actually learn something with you."

"And you will," Jean said firmly. "As long as you keep applying yourself like you did today. There will be boring times. There will be difficult times. But in the end, you will be able to do things that most people only dream of being able to do."

Thaddeus grinned with excitement. "That sounds good to me. I appreciate you teaching me. I know I'm not always the easiest person to be around. People think that I'm completely oblivious to that, but I'm actually more self-aware than people give me credit for. Shocking, I know."

That was surprising to hear and actually a relief. He had to admit that he was one of the people that thought Thaddeus's head was too far up his own ass to notice reality around him and be even remotely aware of how he portrayed himself.

"So what is it you want to gain from all of this? From learning about what kind of magic is actually out there?"

"I want to be able to take myself more seriously, to be honest," Thaddeus said. "I love entertaining people and wowing people, but once I saw what you did when you did that spell to cast the ghosts out of the Winchester Mystery House, I saw how real magic could make people feel. I want to show people that."

"So you want to learn actual magic to profit off of it?" That sounded about right for Thad.

"Not necessarily financial profit, but I wouldn't be opposed to that. I don't want to trick my audience when I show them magic anymore. I want the magic to be real. I want them to really wonder how I did that and not even begin to be able to guess."

That made sense, he supposed. He would be more touched by the notion if it wasn't Thaddeus making it.

"And if you're worried that I am going to spill the beans about magic to the whole world, I won't," Thad said suddenly with a nervous laugh. "After all, a magician never reveals their secrets."

That was comforting.

Jean sat there enjoying his drink and listening to the music of his favorite city. He didn't know if the young man across from him would end up surprising him and be a good student or if he might fail as an apprentice and maybe be a complete waste of time. It was too early to tell, but he tried to be hopeful and just let the sounds of his surroundings soothe his mind.

2

A SEVERE LACK OF BLOOD

It was the duty of the Knights Templar to try to cleanse the earth of the supernatural and the unnatural in their crusade to make the world a safer place. As such, most of them were used to encountering all kinds of strange things. Most commonly, they had hunted down sinful practitioners of witchcraft, but sometimes they would come across less frequent things. They could have to exorcise restless spirits from haunted houses or other such things that most people did not even believe in. But the Knights Templar knew that there was real evil out there and they were devoted to destroying it.

Their swords would slay the evils of the world, and they were well trained to combat their heretic enemies and to have to confront the darkest obstacles. But even with all of their preparation, all of their learning, and all of their practice, there were some things on Earth that still caught them by surprise.

Cedric McKellan was still a fairly new inductee into the

Knights Templar, so he knew there were things that he just had not had the chance to experience yet—but he never expected to see a corpse drained entirely of blood with puncture wounds on its neck.

Given everything he had learned from the Templar, he had a very open mind. He accepted that witchcraft could tap into some sort of real magic, and he had seen the danger it could cause. He also knew from his recent visit to the Winchester Mystery House that spirits of the dead really could linger and cause trouble. Witches, warlocks, and ghosts were real, but for some reason, it was hard to accept that the bloody body at his feet was the victim of a vampire. Vampires were just from stories and seemed somehow much more implausible than the other things he had seen. Immortal beings that had to feed on the blood of the living to survive just seemed ridiculous in reality, no matter how interesting they were in fiction. But, given how unnatural the possibility was, the Knights Templar had to investigate it to see if there was any real merit to it all.

Cedric was ready to write it off before they even got there to see. It just seemed like it would be a waste of time and a pointless exercise, but he figured he should go see just in case there was even a one percent chance that there was any legitimacy to any of it. He doubted it but would prefer to make sure. He wasn't sure what he was really expecting, but the body drained of blood was more than he was expecting.

The coroner he was speaking with looked pale with concern.

"Have you ever seen anything like this before?" Cedric asked, hoping for some kind of rational explanation that did not involve bloodsucking monsters. Then he could go back and tell his superiors in the Templar that this was nothing to be concerned about, and they could move on.

Unfortunately, the coroner did not give him the response that he was hoping for. "No. I've seen all kinds of things but nothing quite like this."

Great, that was a very bad sign.

"But this is not the first one I've heard about recently..."

That was an even worse sign.

"What do you mean?"

"There was talk that something like this happened in Prague a month or two ago and then again in Kiev."

"And are there any theories about what this actually is then?"

"Unfortunately not, but it is scary, isn't it? I really have never seen anything like it...and I've seen some really horrible stuff."

"Aye, you mentioned that."

This was much more than Cedric had anticipated when he started his investigation. Usually, there was at least something he recognized on these kinds of searches. If it were witchcraft, then he would probably find some sort of bones or symbols drawn in blood or even little bags of personal belongings or something of that nature, but this was entirely different. This did not seem like the kinds of things that the Knights Templar would usually handle; for some of his colleagues, the lack of any signs of witchcraft might have been enough to write it off completely. It wasn't their usual brand of strange, but it was still strange anyway. It still seemed worth delving further into.

To determine how he should proceed, he would need to report his findings to his superiors. That was not always the easiest thing to do, especially given recent circumstances. Cedric was still trying to redeem himself in the eyes of his peers, and he wasn't sure that this would be the best way to do it. He would just have to see and hope that the Templar was willing to give him another chance.

The Knights Templar had seen all kinds of horrifying things in their quest to rid the world of witchcraft and dark magic. They had seen rituals involving sacrifice, murders to appease pagan gods, the most gruesome sights that even most police never saw. Still, they seemed shocked when Cedric presented his findings to his superiors. Tristan Malloy, the leader of the Knights Templar, was usually an unshakeable force but even looked perturbed by what was shown. Despite all of the things they had seen, they had not seen anything quite like it.

"So... what new abomination is responsible for this? Someone needs material for some sort of blood magic, no doubt." Tristan clicked his tongue, and all of the other knights listened intently to what he had to say. "The puncture markings on the neck and the victim being drained of blood suggest a rather ridiculous notion, don't they? Vampires perhaps? Ludicrous usually, but there really is no limit to the kinds of hellspawn that find their way into this beautiful world of ours."

The other knights in the room looked unsure whether or not their leader was being serious or if he was actually contemplating that kind of possibility. They all believed in the dangers of magic and witchcraft, but the existence of vampires seemed like it was something that could only ever exist in fiction.

Tristan glanced at all of them. "And this marking...this symbol..." His gaze shifted to Cedric particularly. "Do we have any information on what this is?"

"Not yet," Cedric said. "But I am working on that as well. If I were allowed to continue this investigation, I'm sure I could figure it out and then deal with whatever it is that we are up against."

Tristan and the others all stared at him, and he knew why they were doing so. He was still fairly new to being knighted and fully inducted into their ranks, and his first mission had ended in failure and had included the death of another one of the knights, Arthur, who was respected by all and had been Cedric's mentor. That was not the best first impression to make. None of them hid their disappointment well, and they made it clear that they would have preferred that Arthur be the one to have returned and for Cedric to be dead.

Cedric still felt guilty about all of that, but he couldn't really show it. He couldn't let them know that he had allowed Arthur's killer to live even when he could have killed him with a swing of his sword. The man he spared, Jean-Luc Gerard, was someone that practiced witchcraft, so his life should have been forfeit, but he otherwise seemed like a good person, so Cedric couldn't kill him; even the death of Arthur had just been Jean defending himself. The others could never know that, though, and Cedric still was not quite sure if he regretted that or not. All he knew was that it had resulted in his colleagues looking down on him. He hated that feeling and wanted to prove that he was capable and deserved to be there.

It all depended on Tristan's decision and whether or not he would even allow him to continue this investigation. The leader of the Knights Templar was not an easy man to read.

"Yes, I think you should pursue this further, Mr. McKellan." That seemed to catch most of the other members of the Templar off guard. "I am confident that you are more than capable of getting to the truth of this."

That was nice to hear that he had faith in him even if everyone else did not share that faith. They all looked astounded that Cedric was being trusted to carry out another task after his failure at the Winchester Mystery House. He fed off of their surprise, and it just inspired him to prove all of them wrong.

Tristan gave him his specific orders. "You are to track down the people responsible for these heinous murders and to uncover what all of this means. If it is something evil that should be expunged from the earth, then you must be rid of it. Eliminate the vile heretics, whoever they may be. Do not hesitate."

Cedric nodded. "I won't, sir."

As Cedric left the chamber, he could feel all of the staring resentful gazes boring into him, but he ignored them. He had worked hard to get to where he was in the Knights Templar. A few mistakes on his first assignment did not change that. He was going to make up for what happened. All of his fellow knights would be looking at him differently then. Cedric looked at the ruby ring on his finger and could feel his short sword sheathed in his suit jacket—he had earned those—just like he had earned his knighthood.

This might have been a near-impossible task to take on something that the Knights Templar had never seen before, but he was going to succeed. He had something that the rest of the Templar didn't have: a potential source of information, the same occult expert that he had spared on his first assignment.

Jean-Luc Gerard surviving might have been a mistake, but Cedric would turn that potential error into the key to victory this time. If anyone might know anything about these strange killings, then it was probably Jean. The Knights Templar couldn't know that he was going to a practitioner of witchcraft for assistance, especially the same man that got another knight killed. Cedric would have to be very careful, but he knew that it would be the best move.

So, the next stop he would need to make in his investigation was to go find a bookshop in New Orleans.

As the Templar dispersed and cleared out of the meeting,

an elderly man stopped Cedric before he had a chance to leave and head out on his approved assignment. It was Horace Tolle, keeper of the history of the Knights Templar. He used to be so patient with Cedric and so kind, but in recent weeks, he had joined the others in his resentment. He had become irritable and short with him whenever they interacted. In his old age, he did not seem to even bother trying to hide his disappointment.

"I think Tristan is making a mistake," the old man said glumly—but also quietly, not wanting to be overheard. "You are not ready to go out on your own on something like this. That much is clear. Given what happened, it should be quite some time until you are entrusted with something like this. A mistake."

Cedric was not in the mood to hear it. "Aye? Then how about you go tell Tristan that. Go voice your grievances with him to his face. I dare you."

Horace glowered with those yellowing eyes of his, but he backed down and rubbed his wrinkled face. As expected, he was not willing to actually perform anything even close to insubordination. He grew even quieter.

"Let me ask you, boy... You really think that you will be able to handle this? We don't even know what this is."

"It could be nothing," Cedric said. "But to answer your question, Horace, I am more than ready to handle something like this on my own. I am a member of the Knights Templar just like you. And it's time that people remembered that."

"Perhaps, but myself and the others did not get one of the

finest knights in this order killed on our first assignment. That is the difference, the difference that you seem so willing to just forget about. How convenient that would be if we all shared in your miraculous selective amnesia..."

Cedric turned away and kept walking. He didn't have to explain himself to Horace, and he was tired of being ridiculed for what had happened to Arthur. He was just glad that he had not told them the whole story. Then they would really have reason to hate him. If they were this angry with him for the part he played in not protecting his fellow knight, then they would be even more furious if they knew that he had the chance to avenge him and didn't.

"I am curious, though!" Horace croaked down the hallway. "How is it you intend to proceed on this mystery of yours? Do you have some sort of lead?"

Cedric did not bother turning around to answer him or calling back to the old man. He didn't want to. He did not owe him anything. The success of his assignment would hopefully be enough to convince him and everyone else that he deserved respect in his position.

Did he have a lead? Of course he did. Jean-Luc Gerard would be a great asset, but Horace Tolle and the rest of the Knights Templar had no need to know about any of that. All they would need to do was apologize to Cedric when he came back victorious.

3

AN UNEXPECTED CUSTOMER

Jean hoped that he would never see Cedric McKellan or any of those lunatics from the Knights Templar ever again and especially hoped that he would not see them anytime soon. Unfortunately, he was not that lucky, and his enemies had already flocked to his place of business. Jean played it casually, greeting Cedric like he would any other customer. If the Knights Templar were expecting him to lay out the welcome mat for them, then he was more than happy to disappoint them.

"Good morning. What can I help you with?"

Cedric didn't look overly amused and continued to approach the counter. The last time that the two of them stood that close to each other, Cedric had been trying to execute him with a sword. Jean half-expected that sword to come back out at any minute, but so far, the blade hadn't been drawn—but it was probably sheathed on the inside of

Cedric's jacket just like last time, ready to be wielded if necessary.

"That's far enough," Jean said just to be safe before Cedric reached the register. As fun as pleasantries might have been, Jean was too curious about what the Knights Templar wanted with him. However, it was probably obvious that they wanted him dead for practicing witchcraft. "What brings you to New Orleans, Cedric? I was really hoping that you and I would be staying on opposite hemispheres after what happened, but here you are in my little corner of the city...in my shop. You can probably understand why that might make me a little bit curious, yeah?"

Cedric held up his hands in preemptive surrender. "I'm not here to fight, Jean."

"No?" Jean wasn't exactly convinced. What other reason would he have to be standing there if it wasn't some form of retaliation or him trying to tie up loose ends? Those seemed like the only potential explanations. "You didn't have a change of heart after you let me go, so now you want to finish the job and take my head? Or is it just because your Templar bodies chewed you out and are whipping you back into shape? Is killing me a way to reaffirm your loyalty to them?"

"I'm not here to kill you, Jean," Cedric said calmly. "I'm really not. I didn't tell them much about what happened at that haunted house? I had to tell them about Arthur being killed, but I did not give them any sort of specifics. I didn't want to."

The specifics were that when Cedric and his fellow Templar Knight Arthur tried to kill Jean, he defended himself by using a spell to turn the ghosts haunting the Winchester Mystery House against the Knights Templar. Those spirits tore Arthur apart without any mercy. Cedric tried to avenge his friend but could not bring himself to do it. He apparently was not quite as indoctrinated into the Templar as Arthur was, so he didn't want to kill Jean just for using magic. He let Jean go and probably had a lot of explaining to do about why Arthur was not back with him.

"So what then? They kick you out of your renaissance club because you didn't do what they told you to do? Hate to break it to you, but manipulation like that is pretty common, especially among brainwashing cults."

"The Knights Templar isn't a—you know what, mate? I'm not even going to entertain that discussion. I was not excommunicated for what happened if you really must know."

"Because you didn't tell them that part of it, right?" Jean could see it written all over Cedric's face. "Yeah, you left that little nugget of information out, didn't you, man? Yeah. That was it. Good call, probably. I can't blame you for that. From the sounds of it, that's the kind of thing that they would give you a bit slap on the wrist for. A real big one. So you're cleaning up before they ever even know that it went wrong. Makes sense."

Cedric kept his hands up in surrender and shook his head. "I already told you. I am not here to kill you. I'm really not. You know how you can tell? If I had wanted to kill you, Jean-Luc Gerard, you would already be very dead."

"I don't know about that," Jean said. "You might hesitate and decide to let me go again."

Cedric dropped his arms and looked so sick of the conversation. As rightfully nervous about him as Jean was, he did want to actually hear why he was there then if it was not to kill him. But Jean wasn't going to completely let his guard down around him no matter what his reasons were. He didn't really feel like getting stabbed in the back by a shortsword.

"Fine. If you are not here to murder me, then just what are you doing here, man? Your presence is making me just a little bit on edge, you know? Making me a little jittery, so spit it out then."

"I'm here because I need your help."

"My help?" Jean let out a laugh without meaning to. Out of all of the possible reasons, that was definitely not what he expected to hear. It just didn't sound right at all, not after everything they went through when they first met. "Like you needed my help getting rid of those ghosts in the Winchester Mystery House? And then when I did, you tried to kill me for it."

"Because you used witchcraft—"

"I helped people!" Jean blurted out. "I study witchcraft and magic! I don't usually practice it, but I wanted to get rid of those ghosts and help people, and you punished me for it."

"I'm aware," Cedric sighed. "And that is exactly why I didn't kill you. So yes, I want your help. I want your help because you are exactly the kind of person that might have the answers that I need."

That was certainly interesting. So, Cedric needed to talk to someone that knew their stuff about the occult. Jean absolutely fit that description, but the question was, why would Cedric need an occult expert? Usually, people delving into that kind of topic were the people on the Knights Templar hit list apparently, just like Jean had been.

"So what answers are you looking for exactly? Just in case I'm willing to actually give them to someone like you."

Cedric ignored the remark but looked a bit ashamed. He was probably annoyed that he had to even come to Jean for something. He must have known how awkward of an encounter that was going to be for everyone involved.

"So..." Cedric looked like he was having trouble even asking. He must have been thinking how ashamed all of his other knight friends would be of him. "You study magic and witches and ghosts and all of those paranormal things. Just from looking at this place, I can see that it's practically a library for things like that."

"I forgot how observant you are," Jean said coyly. "Truly remarkable vision there, man."

"So, you know a lot about all of that. But what about vampires?"

Jean thought he misheard the question at first. "What? What do you mean by that?"

"It's just as I said," Cedric said, looking a little embarrassed. "Vampires."

Vampires were a huge part of supernatural lore, especially fiction. They were an extremely popular topic in all kinds of media, but they were not always prevalent in Jean's field of study. Still, he had come across some stuff about vampirism here and there, but that was not usually what he focused on.

"What about them?"

Cedric ran his fingers through his hair like he couldn't believe what he was about to say out loud. "Are vampires real?"

"Real?" Once again, Jean couldn't believe that they were even talking about that. This whole conversation seemed so surreal. It felt like it belonged in some weird dream and didn't quite work inside the actual confines of reality. "And by real, you mean not as intellectual property but as in physically existing? Like are vampires possible? Walking among us and all of that?"

"Precisely."

Jean couldn't help but crack up again, but his cackles didn't seem to deter Cedric. His brows furrowed with annoyance as he waited for Jean to quiet down. His seriousness about all of this actually made Jean even more curious and helped him take things a little bit more seriously. The Templar Knight was not joking around about vampires. These questions came from a place of honesty and legitimacy.

"Do you have reason to believe that vampires exist then?" Jean asked.

"Answer my question first, and I will answer. You didn't say if they were real or not."

"It's a bit of—no, an extremely broad topic. And I admit, it's not something I ever looked into too heavily, but I have seen some. Hell, here in New Orleans, we have our own urban legends about vampires."

"But if you had to hazard a guess...what would you say?"

"I would say I have a very open mind and think it's entirely possible that they exist. Most lore and stories like that come from somewhere. It's just with a subject like vampires, you would have to rifle through centuries of fiction and bullshit to find any sort of truth to it all. In my opinion, some poor soul probably saw a cannibal eating someone, and then their imagination must have run wild with it."

Cedric looked a bit disgusted by that possibility but also looked unconvinced that it was as simple as that.

"So, if I were to tell you that I investigated a body that had been entirely drained of blood with two puncture holes in their neck, what would you say to that? In your expert occultist opinion, of course."

That was very weird and not something Jean ever expected to hear someone actually say. It sounded like something out of some novel, so ridiculous that he almost thought that this was all some kind of elaborate prank or something.

"So you think that some vampire drained this person of all of their blood?"

"I'm not sure what to think, but obviously, that possibility came to mind when I saw the body. Not long ago, I would not have even humored the idea, but after our experience in the Winchester Mystery House and all of the truths I learned with the Knights Templar, I at least wanted to ponder the possibility. So I thought, Who would be the best person to talk to about something like this? Who might know anything about vampires or things like that?"

"Me."

"Yes, that's why I came to you, but you say that you actually don't know much of anything about them, so...maybe I will have to take my question elsewhere."

"I just don't specialize in vampires, but I'm sure I've got books around here going more into detail about the actual lore behind them."

Cedric gave an appreciative nod and glanced around at the shelves. "And you're not talking about any of those Ann Rice vampire novels, are you?"

"No, nothing like that. The books I keep in this shop are one hundred percent legitimate texts. I might be able to find something useful to show you with a little bit of extra time."

Cedric seemed to understand that it was not going to be instantaneous. "How does two days sound?"

"That sounds fine," Jean said. "Not a problem. I can swing that."

"Good. I will return in two days' time and—"

"On one condition," Jean suddenly said, cutting Cedric off.

The young British man practically winced and waited to hear what it was that Jean had to say.

"The condition is that you never show your face in my place of business again after this. This is meant to be a place where the more unexplained things in the world are respected. I think you've made it pretty clear that you are not someone that respects that."

Cedric couldn't deny it. "That is fair, and you are right to make that assumption. And that would be perfect for me because, believe me, I take no pleasure in being in a place like that. I would much rather burn it to the ground." He paused and smiled. "Just a joke, Jean. That's all. I'll be back in two days for whatever you can dig up on vampires."

Cedric turned to leave but then stopped himself.

"Silly me, I had nearly forgotten part of it." He rummaged through his pocket and pulled out a photograph, placing it on the counter so Jean could see. "I was wondering if you had ever come across a symbol like this before."

Jean looked at the picture and was immediately alarmed by its content. It was a still image of a body, presumably laying at a crime scene. The body was pale, and he could see the two incisions on the neck. The odder part and the thing that Cedric was pointing out was the symbol that had been cut into the cadaver's flesh, a little way below the incisions and just beneath the collarbone.

A shape that looked like a V with a vertical line through it had been carved into the corpse.

Jean racked his brain for any memory of anything like that, but the symbol was not exactly unique. It could have meant anything, really. It could have even just been the letter V with an I or a lowercase L through it. It was hard to know for sure.

"I don't recognize it offhand, but I could look into that as well."

His offer seemed to surprise Cedric, but he wasn't going to take the extra steps for his sake. Jean just wanted to figure out how to appease his own curiosity. The fact someone took the time to leave that behind on a victim must have meant something.

"I appreciate that," Cedric said. "Whatever you can find would be helpful."

Cedric left the shop, and Jean was so glad to have him out of his store. It made him feel much better.

Jean just was not sure how he kept getting into these kinds of situations, helping find information for people that he didn't like. First, he had helped Thaddeus with his research on the Winchester Mystery House and was teaching him magic, and now he was going to help a man that tried to kill him become some sort of potential vampire hunter.

Life was strange and full of unexpected surprises that came knocking on one's door.

Once the closed sign was flipped, Jean started to scour his store for anything that had anything to do with vampires.

There wasn't much compared to some of the other books that he collected. Most of those contained information about investigations into ghosts or witches or simply research into things that science could not explain. There was so little on actual vampirism, but Jean wasn't too surprised since most information on the subject was relegated to works of fiction.

He only really managed to find a book about the potential magic involved in someone's blood. So many rituals were centered on the use of someone's blood and its importance. There was power inside of people, and some spells drew on that power. According to that book, that was why vampires needed blood to maintain their immortality. They fed on that power and made it their own. At least, that was what the author of that book had to say in the passages that Jean had read, and they seemed more like theoretical conjecture than anything concrete.

Then there was another book he found about how many cannibals believed that they could tap into more strength than what could usually be attained by feeding on people. Some saw it as absorbing the souls of others and that consumption would grant them that power. That actually went along with Jean's own assumptions on the birth of vampire legends, but again, it really wasn't enough to fully confirm or anything. It was just an interesting connection that Jean had to make on his own since the book itself never even used the word vampire.

The lore of vampires was a muddled mess to begin with. Real or not, there was so much contradiction in their traits, even in fictionalized movies. Sometimes they had fangs, sometimes they didn't, and sometimes those fangs were in a completely different part of their mouth. Sometimes they could be killed by driving a wooden stake through their heart, sometimes it was a silver stake, and sometimes a stake to the heart would not actually do anything to them at all. Sometimes crucifixes and garlic could help repel them, but often they would be useless. Most of the time, they would burn if they were in direct sunlight, but even that had exceptions like that one very popular book that instead chose to have their skin sparkle and crystallize when they stood beneath the sun.

It was hard to find even a shred of truth beneath so much fictional and contradictory lore.

Thaddeus came into the shop in the middle of Jean's research as he usually did after he finished his day performing on the streets of the French Quarter. Jean had hoped that the street magician would stop with all of his parlor tricks now that he was learning about legitimate magic, but Thad argued that his performances were not only something that he loved doing but were also his primary source of income.

Thad took a seat across from him, and he could barely see him over the stack of books that Jean was rummaging through. Thad raised a brow and looked at all of the books with a great deal of curiosity.

"Good evening, Jean. Any reason that you have decided to bury yourself in textbooks on..." Thad picked up one of the snuff books and read the cover. "*Bloodtakers*? So... mosquitos and leeches?"

"Vampires, actually."

Thad's face lit up with excitement. "Really!? Vampires?"

"Yes," Jean said awkwardly. "Why?"

Thad puffed up his chest like he usually did when he wanted to act like he was important and about to start bragging about himself. "I have always been absolutely obsessed with vampires."

"That's good because I don't know all that much about them outside of the usual stuff."

"You are the so-called expert and you don't know about vampires?"

"Of all of the studies that I have done into the occult, the lore of vampires has been the one that interests me the least. It just always seemed so..."

"Amazing?" Thad offered. "When it comes down to it, the legends of vampires have to do with what so many people want. It's all about immortality and the idea of living forever and the price that you are willing to pay to do that. That is what it's really about."

Thad had never looked so interested in their lessons as he did in that moment.

4

THE COMPLICATED HISTORY OF BLOODSUCKERS

Vampires were famous and known throughout the entire world. Everyone knew all about them, either from novels or films. They always had fangs and a craving for blood. They were pale and avoided sunlight. Sometimes they could be driven away by crosses or garlic, and sometimes they could even transform into bats. There were all kinds of different variations, but one thing was agreed on by most people in the world—including Jean—and that was that vampires were not real.

Now there was a chance that that was not actually the case and that they did exist. That was very hard to believe, but Jean knew that supernatural things were entirely possible. He knew from firsthand experience that magic and witchcraft were an actual unexplainable phenomenon that most people did not believe in but he knew to be true. So, there was a chance that vampirism was the same way. It could very well just be something that had been buried by fiction and disbelief but was actually a power that most people were not aware of.

Jean looked through what he did have on vampirism inside of his shop. There was not much, but there was enough to at least find something interesting. Vampires—sometimes in earlier writing spelled as vampyres—were the stuff of legend in many different parts of the world. A lot of cultures had their own versions of undead stalkers of the night that feared the sun and fed on the blood of the innocent. There were all kinds of variations on the myths and legends that people told about creatures like that. Some of the readings made it seem like the legends of vampires started from reports of cannibalism, when some people were drinking the blood of others and feeding on them to survive and extend their own lives. That certainly sounded possible because the basis of it sure sounded like it could be a more realistic version of vampires, before all of the additional things like super strength and fangs and garlic and all of that. Cannibalism did involve feeding on others, and that act could extend someone's own life if they were otherwise starving. And when it came to cannibalism, some cultures thought that feeding on others would give you the strength of those that were devoured or would grant someone enhanced abilities from consuming souls. Maybe that was what some of these strange killings in Eastern Europe now were about. They might have been nothing more than psychopaths eating other people or drinking their blood—realistic cannibalism instead of supernatural vampirism. For a moment, it felt like Jean had cracked the case and was going to have to give the Knights Templar the bad news that the vampires they were looking for were nothing more than people willing to eat their neighbors—but that felt too easy. Things were never that tidy for Jean.

Some of the oldest folklore about vampires came from Europe, where they would come to the homes of grieving families or widows and torment them about their recently deceased loved ones, sometimes taking the shape of their dead relatives and demanding to be invited inside. That was probably where that strange rule about vampires needing an invitation to get inside of a house came from. Jean always thought that it didn't make much sense for vampires to somehow be kept at bay by something like that. If they couldn't get inside without an invitation but wanted something inside of the house, they could always find a more destructive alternative; they could burn down the building or something if they really were that desperate to get what was inside. That must have been where that piece of vampire lore came from, just one of the many examples of the absolute mess that was the history of vampires and where those legends came from.

Jean opened up an old book that chronicled the hysteria in Eastern Europe in the 1800s that involved corpses being staked, and it was after that, that the term vampire became used more frequently in the world. That was helpful to know, but there wasn't much else in the book that seemed like it would really be beneficial.

He put everything that could have had remotely any value aside for Cedric, but it really was not an impressive amount of information. It didn't really need to be, though. He was willing to do the professional thing and give the

Templar some help and the assistance that he had requested, but he didn't need to go out of his way to make sure he had everything he needed. He didn't exactly owe Cedric anything. An argument could be made that he owed him his life after he spared him, but that young Englishman should never have put Jean in that life-threatening position to begin with. Just because he didn't kill him didn't mean that he deserved some kind of prize.

No matter how much he read or any of the things that the books he found said, he still had a hard time even picturing that this venture that Cedric McKellan was undertaking would involve actual vampires. It had to be just some lunatic that was replicating vampiric behavior. That was the only explanation that really made sense to Jean. Time would tell, but he was not very optimistic—which was strange because he usually considered himself to be such an open-minded person.

This was different, though.

Vampires just seemed too far-fetched.

5

JOINING THE MISSION

Cedric McKellan showed back up to pick up his books on the second night after his initial visit, just like he said that he would. He looked anxious as Jean greeted him.

"I take it your superiors don't know where you are right now, right?"

"All they need to know is that I am out there serving them as best as I can, which is the truth. Some of these missions take time and extreme measures."

"And I'm one of those extreme measures then?"

"You are," Cedric said. "Consorting with someone with your proclivities is not something that we like to do or especially make a habit of."

"My proclivities?" Jean asked, trying not to let Cedric's tone bother him too much.

"Practitioners of witchcraft."

"I know what you meant. Usually, you would execute those kinds of people and not work with them, isn't that right? Like you tried to do with me."

"That's right."

"You know how incredibly messed up that is, right? Of course you do. Otherwise, you wouldn't have spared me back at the Winchester Mystery House. No, you are well aware of how wrong the Knights Templar is. Either that or you are just very bad at your job."

"Do you have the books or not?" Cedric asked irritably, avoiding continuing that conversation.

"I do." Jean placed the books in front of Cedric. "There is not much but hopefully something that can help you."

The bell to the front door jingled, and a voice followed, pulling attention away from the conversation.

"Really?" Thad suddenly stepped in. "This is who we were getting all of that information for? Didn't this British guy try to cut your head off back at the Winchester Mystery House? I'm pretty sure that was him, right? What is he doing here?"

Jean tried to explain himself as best as he could. He knew that it must have looked insane from Thad's perspective. "He needed some information, and I agreed to get it for him, just like I got you the information on that haunted house when you needed it. So, I helped him out. That's all."

Thaddeus looked furious and confused, but most of that anger was focused on Cedric. "You are part of that group, right? You are a knight or whatever, isn't that right? That's cool and all, but why are you so interested in vampires? That group you are in get tired of trying to kill people that know magic, so now you have turned into vampire slayers?"

"It's not that simple," Cedric said calmly. "I am just trying to complete an investigation into something that seems like it has something to do with vampires. I wanted to see what Jean knew about it, see if maybe vampires were as real as spirits and witches apparently are."

"So, you and your knight buddies like just getting your fingers in everything then? Like sticking your heads where they really don't belong?"

"You're one to talk, mate," Cedric said with a smirk. "Considering you don't even know any actual magic. That was disappointing. To think that the Templar even considered that you might be someone worth eliminating. What a joke in retrospect, but at least we discovered Jean as a consolation."

"It might have taken me a little while to have my eyes opened, asshole, but they were opened. If you really must know, I've been learning all about the legitimate stuff thanks to Jean. He's been teaching me everything that I wish I had known for years. That I won't have to rely on sleight of hand my whole life."

Jean really wished that Thad had not said any of that, but the street magician just could not help himself. He never missed an opportunity to brag, especially when his ego was being attacked and his abilities questioned. But their arrangement should not have been disclosed so casually. It was bound to upset the Knights Templar, and given the harsh expression that crossed Cedric's face when he heard those words, Jean was right to want to keep his magic lessons under wraps.

Cedric looked to Jean, and his eyes narrowed. "Is that true, Jean? Have you been teaching this buffoon about magic? A private tutor in witchcraft? You cannot possibly be that foolish. I spare your life, and this is what you decide to do with it? You just spread all of your sacrilegious knowledge? Do you have any idea how dangerous that is? Something like that will catch fire, and then the whole world could burn. With the amount of online influence Thaddeus Rose has, how long until his viewers start trying to learn how he's doing magic? A very slippery slope and is really enough to make me think I should have reconsidered killing you—"

"Maybe you should have killed me," Jean growled. "But you didn't. I'm still here. And frankly, I don't owe you anything. I don't have to thank you for what you did. You didn't save me because you were the one that put me in a position where I needed saving to begin with. You chose not to kill me. That's all. There is a big difference between those two things."

"Not in my eyes."

"Of course not. You think I'm indebted to you." Jean patted the stack of books he had put together to give to Cedric. "And if that's the case, here. I have helped you out now when I didn't have to. We're even."

"Your life for a couple of books? I would hardly consider

that even in any sense of the word. Who is to say that these texts will even be helpful to me?"

"They probably won't be," Thaddeus cut in. "Even after picking out those books, he didn't know even close to as much about vampires as I already know without any stupid books."

That got Cedric's attention. "Is that so? You know a lot about vampires then, Thad? Brilliant. Perhaps you are actually good for something after all, but we'll see. So, what more can you tell me?"

"No, no, no, I'm not just going to tell you what I know. If you want my help, then you are going to take me with you."

Cedric looked utterly flabbergasted, and Jean couldn't believe what he was hearing either. "Oh no, that is definitely not going to happen."

"I think you both should come, to be honest," Cedric said. "I could really use the help investigating this. And what better way to do that than to bring people that have much more knowledge about this than I do. In the Knights Templar, we were trained to succeed by any means necessary and to use any tool at our disposal. As much as I don't like you or what you do, I would be lying if I said that it wouldn't be beneficial for me. It would be far more helpful than just reading a couple of old books."

Thaddeus glanced at Jean like he was looking for permission, and Jean just shook his head. "The books are just going to have to be good enough because we are not teaming up with you."

"Of course you would say that, but allow me to rephrase. Help me, and then I will consider us even. I will have spared your life, and you would have helped salvage my reputation among the other knights. We would be square then and only then."

Jean did not like that being held over his head like that, but he should have expected Cedric to pull something like that. As nice as he seemed, Cedric had still been conditioned by the Knights Templar to be a loyal warrior to them. They couldn't forget that or the possible danger that he presented because of that too. Seeing that his pitch did not seem to be quite enough to get Jean to agree, Cedric took a more direct—and openly hostile—alternative approach.

"You can assist me with this now, or I can instead just finish off what I started in that mansion."

That was a very clear threat, and he could tell that Cedric was willing to back his words up. If they refused, he might even pull that sword of his out and kill them right then and there.

Before he knew who he really was, Jean worked with Cedric in the Winchester Mystery House, and they had actually been able to work well together. Perhaps they could work together again; Cedric had proven that he was not as merciless as his brothers in the Knights Templar. Maybe that would be enough reason to be willing to help him. His mercy was the only reason that Jean was even still alive.

"Please," Thad said. "Discovering and proving the existence of vampires would do wonders for my credibility." That was an expected motive for Thaddeus Rose. Anything that could help his fame and his brand would always be his preferred direction to go in. That was not a surprise whatsoever. But he did undeniably know a lot about vampires. Maybe this would be his one chance to really prove his worth.

"Okay," Jean said bitterly. "We will help you investigate this. But we will do it on our terms. If anything happens that I don't like, then we walk away and maybe use our magic to turn you into a frog before we leave."

Jean may have conceded, but he was not done quite yet. He stormed up to Cedric until their faces were practically touching.

"I don't want to hear you ever threaten me again. Is that understood, man? I tend to think I'm a nice guy, but I have my limits. Harming me or people I know is an easy way to end up on the wrong side of my limits. You really want me to use my magic to turn you inside out?"

"No," Cedric said. "Hopefully it won't have to come to that. I'd like to think that I spared your life before for a reason. Maybe this is finally that reason, and God knew that I would need you alive for this part of it. We will leave in a couple days, and you can see exactly what I'm talking about because so much of it needs to be seen to be believed."

Jean nodded. He knew plenty of things that were like that, and that was why he always kept an open mind about things that he heard. The world was full of unexplainable things that would make no sense to most people and that no one would ever believe until they actually saw it with their own eyes. He was fine waiting for that if that was what was needed, but the thing that he was more uncertain about was Cedric McKellan himself. It was one thing to help give him some information, but to spend more time with him was more than just a risk.

"Why didn't you tell me that you were giving those books to that knight guy?" Thaddeus was agitated. He hated being left out of the loop because he could never accept the fact that he didn't have to be involved in every little thing. "That would have been good to know."

"I didn't have to disclose anything to you," Jean said. "I am the teacher and you are the student, remember?"

"This isn't about a lesson. This is about you leaving out the fact that a guy that tried to kill us not that long ago was hanging around just a stone's throw away from us."

"He never tried to kill you," Jean said. "Remember? He and the other Templar were only after people that were actually using witchcraft. Once they realized that you were just a magician with parlor tricks, you no longer mattered to them." Jean knew that saying that would strike a nerve. Being ignored was worse than being killed in Thad's eyes. Sometimes Jean liked to just push his trainee's buttons a little bit just for his own amusement. "But then again, now that you are starting to learn real magic, maybe you will be on their hit list next time."

Thad looked a little bit pleased to possibly be taken seriously in the future but also looked nervous that attention like that could end up with him getting a sword in his belly. He was definitely thinking about the possibilities and wasn't sure how to react exactly.

"You really think that they would come after me?"

"It's possible," Jean said teasingly. "I'm honestly surprised that they have not already taken the head of the great and all-powerful Thaddeus Rose."

Thad's face grew red, and he shook his head. "Ha. Ha. Very funny. So, are we really doing this, though? Please tell me that this is all some clever ruse or something and we are just going to kill the guy in his sleep before he kills us..."

"We are not going to kill him," Jean said. "And I don't think that he is going to slit our throats in the middle of the night either."

"That does not sound like a guarantee," Thad said, his voice quivering a little bit.

"Welcome to the real world, Thad," Jean said. "A place where there are no real guarantees or certainties and where sometimes the only way to achieve anything is to take a risk. This is a risk, for sure, but it could be very beneficial for us in the long run."

"You are not just giving in and helping him because he threatened us?"

"Of course not," Jean said. "I'm not exactly all that afraid of the Knights Templar. You seem to have forgotten that I already killed one of them before he had a chance to kill me."

"Yeah, but that's because of the ghosts in the Winchester Mystery House."

"The ghosts that *I* summoned and managed to wrangle with magic, yes. They would not have done that if not for the incantation that *I* invoked."

Jean didn't know why he was getting into an argument about ego with Thaddeus Rose. There was no point in trying to have Thad admit that he got any credit. The street magician was not the kind of person that liked to share the glory with anyone or acknowledge the accomplishments of other people. That just was not his way. Jean was also not being entirely honest with his student about the threat that the Knights Templar posed. He could pretend that they were not a big deal or act like he could handle them without issue, but that was not entirely true. Jean just needed Thad to be calm and levelheaded, and he wouldn't be if he was terrified of who they were going to have to work with. This was a lesson to him, to keep calm and not jump to conclusions or rush into action.

"Are you going to help me out with this one, or are you too afraid to?" Jean asked, knowing exactly how to convince Thaddeus Rose to do something. All he had to do was question his capabilities, and Thad's ego would not be able to handle that and would become obsessed with proving him wrong. It was actually very simple. "Because if you're afraid, you can stay here. I will give you some reading to do while I'm gone."

"Of course I'm going!" Thad hissed. "Obviously! You said yourself that you barely know anything about vampires.

I'm not going to miss the chance if this really is something like that. No chance in hell."

"Good," Jean said, happy that his plan worked perfectly, as he knew it would. "So, make sure to tie up any loose ends you have here for now. Hopefully, you will learn far more from this opportunity than you could from any of the books in here."

Thaddeus nodded with some relief and enthusiasm. The street magician hated being cooped up in the bookshop. He preferred to be more hands-on or at least be out in public where he could have a potential audience; he enjoyed things like that much more than he enjoyed having his face buried in a book.

"We will prepare, and then we will meet up with Cedric when we're ready to go. Hopefully, we won't be walking into a trap. That would be a shame."

Thad's anticipation wavered a little bit with fear, but he gave a nod and hurried out of the shop to go get ready for their trip.

Jean looked around at his bookstore, still startled by the turn of events. When Cedric McKellan had spared him in the Winchester Mystery House, he thought—and hoped—that they would never see each other again. Instead, now they would be in each other's lives again. Jean just hoped that this was not just going to be another chance for Cedric to try to run him through with that Templar sword, but he also had to be ready in case it was.

He had to hope for the best but be ready for the worst.

Thaddeus was excited by the prospect of taking part in this potential journey that had been brought to him and Jean. His tutelage under the occult expert was already paying off, and he was getting the kind of experience that he was hoping to get from learning from him. It may not have been magic lessons, like making things levitate, but traveling the world in search of a vampire was much more exciting than sitting in the shop and reading a bunch of books. A field trip was exactly what he needed as a student.

The only problem was that he needed to let his usual crew know. Kaleb and Dani had been his people for a long time now, the kind of friends that he could rely on to support him in his dream to become a world-famous magician. Dani was his patient handler and Kaleb his trusted cameraman. He appreciated more than he sometimes let on, but they hadn't been spending as much time together lately, not since he started his lessons with Jean. But, he still wanted to let them know about what was going on.

The two of them were hanging out in the café in the French Quarter that they usually enjoyed. They had even saved a seat for Thad like they usually did. That was nice of them, but he wouldn't be staying for long.

"Well, look who decided to actually show up," Dani said with a little laugh. "Thought you would be over at Hogwarts right now."

"We're actually heading out of the city soon."

"Really?" Kaleb asked, looking excited. "Where to?"

"Eastern Europe. We're investigating killings where the victims are drained of blood. Could be vampires—I hope it's vampires."

Both of his friends looked very interested now, practically leaning forward over the table. Kaleb asked the obvious question. "Can we come?"

Thad expected that and hated being the bearer of bad news. In situations like that, they were usually right there with him, and that was what he wanted. He needed Dani to help keep him in line, and he needed Kaleb and his camera to make him look good. Their help was essential in getting Thaddeus Rose's name out there to an audience, but this wouldn't be one of those times. Since it involved the Knights Templar and top-secret feuds involving the supernatural, it had to be kept much more under wraps and kept away from the limelight.

"Sorry, guys. Not this time."

Dani and Kaleb both looked flabbergasted by his rejection. They glanced at one another with some disappointment and confusion and even looked a bit annoyed to be told that they were not getting an invitation. They were probably wondering why he had even bothered to tell them about it then.

"I just wanted to let you guys know that I was going to be gone for a bit, with Jean."

"So, he's your new best friend then?" Kaleb asked with a mix of humor and actual resentment. "A couple magic lessons and you kick your old pals to the curb?"

"You know it's not like that. Tell you what, when I get back, we are going to start hanging out more again. I'll make sure that we make time."

"Fair enough," Dani said. "So when will you be coming back exactly?"

"I'm not really sure," Thad said honestly. "Hopefully it won't be too long."

"It's kind of important for me to know your schedule, Thad. How am I supposed to book you anything good if I don't even know if you will be able to be there?"

"I'm sorry, we'll figure that out whenever I get back."

"*If* you get back, you mean," Kaleb cut in. "Being around Jean tends to end with a lot of danger. Remember everything that happened at the Winchester Mystery House? We all almost died."

"But thanks to Jean, we didn't, right? And we got all of the credit for it, remember? Jean's probably the safest guy to be there with. None of what happened there was his fault. We were the ones that asked him to go to that haunted house to begin with."

Dani and Kaleb both settled down a little bit. They probably would enjoy more alone time together, so they should really have thanked him for giving them that opportunity. They would be just fine without him for a little bit.

"Just be careful, alright?" Dani said. "You won't have us to watch your back this time."

"I'll be fine," Thad said. "I'm Thaddeus Rose, remember? I have nothing to fear from anyone."

That didn't seem to put either of his friends at ease. They would see when he got back that he had succeeded and would probably grow even more during the journey—at least he hoped he would.

6

EXPERIENCING A REAL PROPHECY

As always, Jean wanted to get a bit of a heads-up on what to expect if he was leaving New Orleans. There was only one place where he could really do that. He would have to pay a visit to the old fortune-teller Mama May.

Unlike every other time he went to get a glimpse of his future, he decided to bring a guest this time. It would be good for Thad to experience an actual clairvoyant at work since he so proudly had put that on his business card when he barely knew what it was. It could help in stripping away all of that fraudulent pomposity and make Thaddeus understand real magic more. Thad, however, did not seem all that excited to be going there.

"Everyone always talks about Mama May and how great she is. You can throw a rock anywhere in the French Quarter, and you are probably going to hit someone that has praised her."

"That's because she is worth all of the praise. She has quite the gift, as you will see for yourself."

Thad looked skeptical. "I don't know. I've never been a big fan of fortune-tellers or mediums or mind readers or any of that. Psychics are usually just trying to scam you. Predicting the future and all of that is usually just bullshit. They look for tells on a person and extrapolate information or sometimes even do background checks on their guests. That's how they seem to know about you. A bunch of frauds, really."

"You're going to call someone else a fraud?" Jean could not help but laugh at the irony of that. "When you have spent your career tricking people into believing that you are performing magic when you are not?"

"Magician techniques are an art form. It's about amazing an audience. I'm not preying on people's anxiety about the future or the unknown."

That was a decent enough point, but it was just strange that Thaddeus was the one making it.

"You're not entirely wrong, though. Most of the psychics and fortune-tellers in the world are full of shit but not Mama May. She is the real deal, the realest that I have ever seen."

"I guess I'll just have to see for myself. If anyone will be able to tell if she's using some kind of trick, it'll be me."

Jean wasn't worried about that. He knew that Mama May's prophecies were not any kind of subterfuge. He had experienced her accurate predictions many times. The last time he consulted her was when he was on his way to the Winchester Mystery House when she warned him that a man with a sword was going to try to kill him, and sure enough, that was exactly what had happened; she had a vision about the Knights Templar coming after him, and according to her, Cedric was going to be his doom someday. So maybe he shouldn't be working with Cedric and instead should be as far away from him as possible.

Mama May was usually asleep by that point in time, but he was sure that she would be willing to make an exception for him. Jean had known that old crone since he was a kid, and she had seemed old even then. She was one of the staples of the supernatural community in New Orleans. She had seen all kinds of people come and go for decades, so she would see Thaddeus as the street hustler that most of the educated people in the city saw street magicians as anyway. Hopefully, his teaching could steer Thad in the right direction. Hopefully, she didn't mind a little extra company.

Jean went up to her back door as he usually did and found that it was locked, so he tapped his knuckles against it a few times. He could hear shuffling inside of the house, and then the familiar old woman opened the door and looked at them with sleepy eyes. She appeared as frail as she always did, like a strong wind would be enough to knock her over, but that tiny body of hers had rather remarkable power.

When she saw Jean, she rolled her eyes and sheepishly waved them inside. "What trouble have you found yourself in now, Jean-Luc Gerard? Or what new trouble are you trying to avoid? Even without seeing, I can tell you that you should just be more careful and you would not have this problem."

"And why do you think I'm in trouble, Mama?"

"Because that is the only time that you come to see me. That is the only reason you would ever be here, and with a stranger no less."

Jean gestured toward Thad. "I'm sorry, Mama, let me introduce you. This is Thaddeus Rose."

"Aw yes, Thaddeus Rose. The street magician?"

Thad looked a little alarmed and impressed. "Either you're a fan, or wow, your psychic stuff is impressive."

"It has nothing to do with my psychic 'stuff' at all, child. People come to me for all kinds of reasons, and people also talk. And I have heard nothing good about the name Thaddeus Rose. You are known for putting on quite a show but completely disgracing all of the actual users of magic that have come before you."

Thad looked offended and opened his mouth to speak, but Jean was quick to cut him off before he had the chance to say something embarrassingly stupid.

"I have been teaching Thaddeus about true magic and hopefully that will show him a better way."

Mama May gave a stiff, unconvinced nod. "So, you are here to see what may happen then? As always?"

"Yes," Jean said. "I am to undertake another trip, and given how chaotic the last one was, I think some foresight into what to expect could be a big help in the long run. I also wanted to show Thad a real fortune-teller at work."

Mama May grimaced. "I am not an animal to be observed at a zoo, Jean-Luc Gerard."

"I know, Mama, I just thought it would be a good bit of experience for him. So that's why he is here."

"If he wants a real good look at it, then perhaps I should do a reading for him and he can experience that kind of magic firsthand..." Mama May's stare shifted to Thad. "That is, if you are willing to put yourself through that...if you are not afraid of would the future might hold."

Thad straightened his posture to try to look as unintimidated as possible. "What the future might hold? Isn't the whole point of your job to show me what the future will hold? What's with all of this 'might' stuff?"

Most people knew why Mama May had gotten her name and where it came from. Mama May could see glimpses of possible futures, but there was no guarantee. It just showed her what could potentially happen. That might make people wonder what the point was, but Jean had experienced firsthand one of her possible futures actually coming to pass, and he had been grateful for some warning.

"I can see what may happen, but the future is never solidified or written in stone. One small change can completely alter everything. I can tell you what a possible future could be so you could try to avoid it or perhaps try to take the proper actions to make it happen. Anyone that tells you that any future is destined to happen is a fraud.

That is one easy way to tell the fakes from the legitimate clairvoyants."

Thaddeus nodded, letting that notion sink into his head. "I'm not afraid to hear what might happen to me. I'm sure it will be all good things."

"We shall see. Come, let us sit and find out."

Mama May led them into her living room, where she usually did her predictions. She sat in her seat, and Thad took the seat across from her, with a small table between them. It was a familiar sight for Jean. He had been in that position many times, and he watched as Mama May began her ritual.

The old woman picked up her thin knife, and Thad immediately threw up his hands in a panic. "Whoa, whoa, whoa! What the hell is that thing for!?"

"I will need to be in contact with your blood in order for the ritual to work."

Jean didn't usually give that part of it much thought, but after some of the books he had looked through recently, that part about the blood stood out way more. It was another example of blood having power of its own. So, there might have been some truth to that aspect of vampirism after all.

Mama May poked the tip of the blade into Thad's palm, and he yelled out dramatically, really milking the pain. Jean knew firsthand that that part of it didn't hurt that badly. That was typical of Thaddeus Rose, though. He liked to make things as dramatic as possible. When Mama May took hold of his bleeding hand and squeezed, he reacted just as viscerally as when he got poked. He seethed with pain as she squeezed and blood started to spill between his fingers.

Mama May's eyes rolled back, and she fell into her usual trance as she started to see whatever possible future could be heading his way.

"You are defined by your ambitions, but your ambitions are always out of reach. Soon they will be closer to you than they have ever been. But it will not be an easy road to get there. You will face things that you once believed did not exist. You will face death, and you will face your greatest fear. You worry that your name will never be remembered and will be forgotten as easily as most names are. If you want to be immortalized and remembered, then you will have to open your mind and accept the things you once never would.

"But, I see something else too. Yes, to fulfill your ambitions, you will have to swim. Yes, you will have to swim through a red pool, a lake of blood, the blood of many. You must be careful, though, for if you drown, then your greatest fear will come true, and no one will ever remember your name. No one."

Mama May squeezed harder, and Thad tried to stand up and pull away from the old woman, but he couldn't get out of her grip.

"Swim carefully in that blood, Thaddeus Rose. Stay afloat. Or sink and be forgotten. Forgotten. Utterly forgotten."

Mama May's eyes settled, and she let go of Thad. He fell

backward onto the floor, holding his bloody hand and stammering in a panic. Sweat rolled down his face, and he looked at the old woman like she was some abomination that he should be terrified of.

"What...what was all of that!? What were you talking about!?"

"Your future, child. I was talking about your future, of course."

Thad slowly started to stand up on trembling legs. "But what did you mean by all of that? All of those things you were talking about, like the pool of blood that I have to...that I have to *swim* through? What did you mean by all that?"

"I meant exactly what I said. I can only get glimpses of those days that might be ahead of you. I tell you what I see, and it is up to you to act on that information...or don't."

Thaddeus looked absolutely shell-shocked by the premonition. If he was not a believer in Mama May before, he definitely was now.

"How about you, Jean-Luc Gerard? You came to see what may be on its way to you as well, yes?"

"I did," Jean said and looked at Thad. "You will be alright. The first one is always the worst one. Considering you will be joining me on this trip, she might see the exact thing for me. Maybe I will be swimming through the pool of blood with you then, man."

That didn't seem to put Thad's mind at ease, and he still looked absolutely overwhelmed by everything that had happened. It wasn't a comfort to know that he might be swimming through blood in the near future, even if Jean was going to be doing it beside him.

Jean took the seat where Thad had been sitting across from Mama May. The old woman cleaned off her knife to get ready to restart the ritual. Purdue wouldn't make nearly as much of a scene about it as Thaddeus had. He was more than used to the way that she did things. He knew that the scarier part was the things that she said. Hopefully, she would be giving him some good news this time.

After she pricked his hand and took it in her own hands, she closed her eyes, and he could feel the visions making her frail little body quiver. She was starting to see something. There was no doubt about that. Mama May's grip tightened, and she winced.

"Things have not changed much for you. I still see him. The shadow with the gleaming sword. I see him standing over you. Even still. He stalks you, and he remains the end of your life."

That was not exactly new information. She had already warned him that Cedric would bring ruin upon him, so it wasn't very shocking to hear again. The fact that Cedric was going to be working with him more made it scarier. It increased the chance of that coming to pass. Or perhaps it gave Jean time to change that and to persuade Cedric not to try anything.

"But the swordsman will not be the only thing that will be trying to hurt you. There are men in red robes, and they want to carve you up. They want to take what is inside of you and drink from your soul."

That sounded like people were after his blood, trying to devour him—so eerily like vampires if there was any truth to that.

"You also stand in the pool of blood, and that red will flood through your life until there is nothing but blood everywhere. But the shadow with the sword has laid claim to you, so also comes for you. A rescuer may save you from drowning in your own blood only to end your life themselves and take your blood anyway."

So, it sounded like there were two threats that Jean was going to have to navigate around. There was the shadow with the sword, which was probably Cedric or maybe some other member of the Knights Templar. That was one of those threats, and the other threat was apparently some group of people in red robes that wanted to devour him. And according to this, one of these threats might save him from the other only to stab him in the back.

Mama May's hand shook a little, and she clenched her teeth. "It's in the blood. The key. The key is in the blood. In the bl-bl-blood. Yes. In the blood."

Jean wasn't sure exactly what she meant, but it confirmed that he must have been on the right track when it came to thinking that the blood was more important than most people thought. Those books he had chosen had definitely put him on the right track. Now he just needed to keep going down that path until he figured out what exactly was going on.

Mama May pulled away and let out a tired sigh. "Things still seem so dark for you, Jean-Luc. I was hoping to see something brighter for you."

"You know me, Mama. I have always had a habit of getting mixed up in all kinds of trouble."

That had always been true, and Mama May was well aware of that. So, she shouldn't have been too surprised that he kept getting himself into danger.

Thaddeus Rose seemed to have calmed down a little and looked at Mama May with more respect than he had when they first got to her place of business. He looked a little more at ease but also a bit more petrified at the same time, realizing just how real the psychic abilities of Mama May were.

"It sounds like we are just going to be having a real rough time in the near future then?" Thad said. "Because none of that sounded very positive."

"I wish I had better news to give you," the frail woman said. "But I only saw violence for you two. Still, things are not entirely hopeless. As I have said and as Jean-Luc well knows, the things that my magic allows me to see are only possibilities. They can be avoided and altered. Rivers that can be rerouted entirely and flow in a completely new direction."

Jean turned to Thaddeus. "You see what real magical ability can do? Nothing in your bag of tricks can do anything like that now, can it?"

Thad had to concede on that one. He had never seen

anything quite like it. It seemed like he was still just trying to process what he had just been given a chance to witness. Actual magic was sometimes very difficult for a human brain to rationalize.

Mama May offered them a thin smile. "Good luck with whatever it is that you are doing, Jean-Luc, but don't be surprised if you see some blood on your travels. The future seems stained with it."

That was the part of those prophecies that stood out the most to Jean. The talk about the pool of blood or people in robes wanting to take their blood sounded particularly dark and not at all good. Jean was not squeamish around blood or anything, but nobody wanted to have to swim through it like Mama May had said that they would have to do. He hoped that she was being metaphorical.

The most alarming part of it all was that Mama May's words aligned with all of the research that Jean had been doing recently. It all seemed to coincide perfectly with everything he had been reading about vampires and the power of blood. That could mean that Cedric and the Knights Templar really were on the trail of something like that. If that was the case, then for all they knew, they were walking right into a vampire nest—then they would know for sure if those monsters were real or not.

At least they knew to have their guard up, no matter what kind of threats they were going to be facing.

"Thank you, Mama May," Thad said. "I'm sorry that I doubted you. It won't happen again."

"Just keep an open mind, child. That is where real power can be found."

"So, she really was the real deal then. You weren't kidding around about that. I'm still trying to wrap my head around it."

As they walked through the night, Jean could practically hear all of the gears twisting and turning inside of Thad's head. He was thinking back on what had just happened, trying to figure out what exactly he had just witnessed. But no matter how hard he tried, he couldn't quite figure it out.

When someone witnessed something that shouldn't be possible, their brain did everything it could to try to make sense of it, and if it couldn't, it would instinctively register what had happened as not being possible. It would deny the reality it had seen, and the person would make excuses for it, writing it off as not being possible. That was just how people worked, but it was always interesting to see someone try to make sense of something that just was not supposed to make sense.

Even with everything that Thad was reading in his studies, he still seemed completely flabbergasted by the firsthand display that Mama May gave.

"She was not making any of that up, was she?"

"No," Jean said. "Mama May can be trusted. But just don't count on it coming true."

"I know, I remember what she said. It's just one possible future that might not happen. Still, I should probably be a little bit worried about it, shouldn't I? I mean, I don't really want to drown in blood. That isn't something I signed up for."

"Then avoid red pools or red ponds, and you will be fine."

"You make it sound so easy, but from the sounds of it, you might be swimming through it with me. And then what she said to you. So, Cedric might try to kill you with that sword again or some guys in red are going to try to hurt you first. That all sounds really bad. Worse than mine, really. Who do you think the guys in red are?"

"If I had to take a guess...given the current path we're going down, it's probably the group that is carving that mark into people and taking their blood. The Dracule or whatever. I would put money on it being them."

"So, by going after them, we might be setting ourselves up to be stabbed or drowned. This all sounds so promising. I'm so glad we went to Mama May so I can be terrified by what is coming our way."

"I told you. Don't be too freaked out by what she said. You can't dwell on it too much. For all you know, it might not actually happen at all. Then you would have freaked yourself out for nothing. We will meet Cedric tomorrow and figure out a plan from there."

"And you really trust him not to kill us?"

"Of course I don't. The Knights Templar wants everyone that uses magic to be killed. I don't think that's changed. I think Cedric had a moment of clarity—but in their eyes, weakness—back at the Winchester Mystery House. But he probably got reamed for what happened. I'm sure he's looking to correct his mistake. He's just going to use us for all we are worth before he finishes what he started. And from what Mama May said, I'm probably not wrong about that."

"It's just that those blood cult people could get to you first."

"I know, I know. But the best way to find out what the future holds is to just go experience it and see what happens. So let's do that."

7

THE FAITH OF A KNIGHT

Cedric felt his phone ringing and knew exactly who it was that was trying to reach him. It was his superiors in the Knights Templar checking in on him. He knew that they would be keeping a closer eye on him. They wanted to be extra cautious and get updates from him regularly since his first assignment at the Winchester Mystery House did not go quite as well as he had hoped it would. They wanted to make sure mistakes were not made again.

Cedric was going to do his best not to fail again and use any means at his disposal to succeed—including using someone like Jean-Luc Gerard. The Knights Templar did not need to know how he succeeded as long as he did. So he would keep his alliance with Jean quiet. The other Templar would not understand how useful it could be to have practitioners of magic assisting them. They would just want people dead, no execrations and no matter how beneficial they could be to their cause. The Knights

Templar's crusade to eliminate witchcraft and the supernatural was a bold one, but the narrow-mindedness of how they went about that could sometimes be more of a detriment than a strength. They needed to be more adaptable and flexible if they wanted to fully succeed.

He picked up the phone. "This is Cedric."

"Aw yes, Mr. McKellan." He recognized the voice immediately as Edmund Foley, one of his superiors in the Knights Templar and the one to have given him the assignment of looking at the recent murders to begin with. Edmund was notoriously resolute in maintaining the codes and duties of the Templar and followed them to the letter. He was exactly the kind of person that would be against the idea of working with an expert on the occult, so he was also exactly the kind of person that Cedric would not talk about it with. Edmund would not understand. It was as simple as that.

"How is your assignment going? Better than your last one went, I hope." Edmund liked to make fitting remarks, anything that would make other people feel uncomfortable and make himself feel superior. That was just how he was and always had been.

Cedric played along and was glad Edmund couldn't see his face. "Better than the last."

"That is very good to hear. Arthur was a dear friend of mine, so you can imagine how hard it was to hear that he had been killed in some American haunted house."

"I'm sorry." That was all Cedric could say over and over to

his fellow knights without giving them more specifics. "I wish I had been able to save him in time."

"It is just unfortunate that a knight as experienced and as skilled as Arthur was, had to fall. You have very large shoes to fill, and I hope you will not disappoint. Arthur was your mentor, and you were the last one to see him alive, so you must also be the one to carry on his legacy properly."

Cedric still felt guilty about not avenging Arthur, but he just could not kill Jean at the time when it was all happening. Jean had very clearly just been defending himself, and nothing he had done had seemed overtly malicious and worthy of execution. It was complicated, and Cedric was still not exactly sure how he felt about all of it in the grand scheme of things.

"We would like an update on your progress, if you please."

That was a poorly hidden code for "we want to make sure that you have not messed anything up," and Cedric knew that. So, he made sure to tell them exactly what they wanted to hear and to leave out the parts that they didn't.

"I am currently following a trail to Romania after I found the information detailing the origin of that mark carved in the body." He just wasn't going to say where he had gotten that information from. What the Knights Templar didn't know wouldn't hurt them.

"And?"

"It has to do with a cult connected to Vlad the Impaler, so we are going to his homeland and seeing what we can find out."

There was a pause on the other end. “Who is we?”

Cedric froze, and panic raced through his mind. He had to act quickly and fix such a foolish mistake. “I meant me—I mean, I meant *I*. I am heading to Romania. I guess when I said we, my brain was thinking about the pilot and all that.”

“Ah, I see.” It was hard to tell if Edmund was convinced by his voice alone. “Well, keep us posted with what you find there.”

“I'll do that.” However, he was only planning on giving them updates when he absolutely had to. They didn't need to stay in the loop. He would get the job done and show them all that he didn't need his hand held.

This was Cedric's assignment to complete, and he was going to do it his way.

“I'm surprised that you have allowed Cedric McKellan to go try to do this on his own.”

Three of the top members of the Knights Templar stood alone in a private chamber, far away from where their subordinates and fellow knights could hear the conversation. It was a much-needed conversation, especially given the recent meetings and assignments within the organization.

Horace Tolle was careful with his words like he always was. The old man had lived a long enough life to know when to pick his battles and to know how hard he should fight when he decided to actually partake in one. He was always careful when he spoke to the grandmaster of the Knights Templar, always careful with what he said to Tristan Malloy.

He stood with Edmund Foley, who had just gotten off of the phone with Cedric and who shared Horace's reservations about the decision that had been made.

Their leader, Tristan, stood casually as he always did. He was as well dressed as ever and kept his hands in the pockets of his expensive suit. He listened calmly like he always did, but they knew that Tristan never stopped thinking. He was always concocting some sort of plan in his mind, quietly contemplating his options as others tried to speak to him. This was one of those times and was part of the reason that the old man was so careful with him.

"I agree with Horace," Edmund said. He was a bit brasher than Horace and a bit more willing to speak his mind and voice his concern with their leader. Edmund was well respected within the Knights Templar, and there were plenty of knights that would have probably preferred that he be in charge instead of Tristan, but they would never actually speak those thoughts aloud. "Arthur is dead because of that boy. He was knighted and inducted into our ranks, and the first thing he did was make a mistake that killed one of our best. For all we know, that was a calculated move, and Cedric is trying to dismantle us from the inside out."

"I highly doubt that," Tristan said calmly. "And that kind of hyperbole and exaggeration is dangerous. Those are not the best thoughts to have and can seep into your mind until you cannot even think straight, Edmund. Be careful with that line of thinking. Cedric McKellan made a mistake, you are not wrong about that, and as much as I wish that he had not made that mistake, he cannot take it back. Arthur is dead, yes, but Arthur also knew the risks. We all know the risks of serving this order, and we are willing to give our lives to the Templar. Mistakes happen, and sometimes people die. I will not punish Cedric for it. If anything, Arthur should have been experienced enough to survive. Some of the blame falls on himself...may he rest in peace."

"That may be so," Horace said. "But this sounds like something that we have never seen before, something that might change our entire crusade as we know it. You are really entrusting something that important to a novice who has impeded us more than he has actually helped us?"

"All I have done is give Cedric McKellan another chance to prove himself to us. Because of what has happened and where he stands right now, he will try harder than most to succeed. If anything, that young man is the perfect candidate to handle something like this. He will tackle it with more tenacity because he has more to lose and more to prove. He will do fine."

"And how do you think he will manage that?" Edmund growled. "He has refused to give us any indication of what his actual plans are and has done very little to give us any peace of mind at all. How can we have faith in him when he does not even seem to have a plan?"

"You use the word faith so wistfully, my friend," Tristan said, "when faith itself so often relies on what we do not know and on things that are not able to be seen. Just because we cannot see a way for him to succeed does not mean that he won't, and it does not mean that we should doubt him. Faith is often based on nothing but hope and belief. Cedric McKellan may disappoint us once again, and if so, we will decide what happens to him then. But he deserved another chance. And that is the end of it. Both of you: I will hear no more about this until he returns victorious or in defeat. From there, we can talk again. But for now, have faith in your fellow knight and hope for his success."

Horace Tolle and Edmund Foley grew quiet and nodded to their leader. They knew that once Tristan ended a conversation, it meant that there was no conversation anymore. There was no point trying to get him to hear them anymore, and they would just have to believe in Cedric. Neither of them was convinced to have faith in the young knight, but they were convinced to keep quiet about their doubts, at least for now. Time would tell whether or not they were right to doubt his abilities.

Cedric would not have been surprised if Jean-Luc Gerard and his new protege did not show up to meet with him. After all, the last time they had worked together ended with them as enemies. They had every reason not to trust him and to think that this alliance was nothing more than a ploy to then stab them in the back. He would not fault them if that was what they believed, but he was relieved when he saw them approaching, ready for the journey ahead.

"It is good to see you," Cedric said honestly, shaking Jean's hand before shaking Thaddeus Rose's. Both men looked rightfully uneasy, but he did his best to make them feel better about everything. He needed them to be at their best if they were going to be assets in helping him complete this assignment. Jean-Luc Gerard alone had a lot to offer, but he could not say the same for Thaddeus Rose; that street magician would probably just be dead weight, but Cedric would be happy to be proven wrong about that.

More than anything, he wanted to prove himself to the Knights Templar, even if it meant doing it in a way that they would never approve of. Working with an occult expert would give him an edge that his peers never even dared to consider.

"It's good to see you too," Jean said, but he probably was not very sincere about that. What he said next proved that much. "It is especially good that you haven't put a sword up to my throat already, you know what I mean?"

"I don't plan to do that again," Cedric replied, and meant what he said. "You don't have to worry about that. If I had wanted to kill you, I could have, and if I still wanted to kill you, then I would. That is really what it comes down to, so you have nothing to fear from me."

"That's good!" Thaddeus Rose said, letting out a loud breath of relief. "I really don't want to get impaled by a sword."

"You won't," Cedric said. "I don't have any ill will toward either of you, no matter what the rest of the Knights Templar say. I know that I am supposed to purge the world of people like you, but I like to think with my own mind more than that. By all accounts, I should have killed you that day in the haunted house, Jean, but I didn't, and I am living with that decision. And the best part about that decision is that you could be a valuable help to me."

Jean laughed. "Ah, I see now, man. You spared me so you could use me as a tool. That makes sense."

Cedric did not mean for it to come out that way, but he also couldn't deny that he was mostly right about that. Jean-Luc Gerard was not his friend, and they were probably never going to be, but he would be of a lot of assistance with all of the things that he knew about the occult.

"You're not wrong," Cedric said with a laugh of his own. "So, are you ready?"

"As ready as we are going to be," Jean said.

"Good. I have a private jet being readied for us to depart."

Thaddeus Rose's eyes lit up. "A private jet!? I didn't know that you were rich! Talk about luxury!"

"Being a part of an ancient order of knights has its benefits, aye."

8

FLIGHT WITH A FORMER FOE

The private jet was impressive, but Jean expected as much since it had the financial backing of the Knights Templar. An organization that had existed as long as the Templar probably had a lot of money and a whole lot of resources as well.

Cedric must have noticed Jean examining the jet because he spoke up about it. "A lot of time, we like to take regular commercial flights and blend in more, but for things like this, where we could be running all around the planet, it's more convenient to have your own wings instead of relying on others."

"I guess that makes sense, yeah. Well, I appreciate the lift. Not all of us have an order of witch-hunting knights taking care of us. Private jets aren't something that I can usually just come by normally."

Cedric sat down beside him and pulled out the familiar picture of the corpse with the bite marks and the symbol on the body. It wasn't an image that Jean loved to look at, but he kept having to see it anyway over and over again.

"So, someone is killing people, draining all of the blood from their bodies and leaves behind two incisions on the neck and carves that mark into their bodies." Cedric got right to the point. That about summed it up. "Do either of you magical experts have any theories about all of this that you would like to share?"

"Vampires, probably," Thad said from where he lay back in his seat. "It has to be vampires."

"It's not vampires. We know that it's connected to a cult," Jean said. "The motive is what we can't really be sure of yet. They are enacting some kind of vampiric fantasy, it seems."

"Vampires!" Thad called out again.

"Vampiric!" Jean called back across the jet. "That does not necessarily mean that they themselves are undead creatures. This could be a sick joke or perhaps some kind of ritual. The work of a delusional mind. It can be any number of things."

"Or it could be a vampire."

This was the kind of thing that made Jean not want to go anywhere with Thaddeus Rose in public. He would sacrifice any kind of in-depth conversation just for the chance to make some kind of annoying remark.

Jean decided to change the subject and ease the tension in the jet.

"So, we have some time to kill, right? It might be a perfect time for you to tell me more about the Knights Templar and why you love them so much."

"I am not going to do that."

"No? Why not? We are all friends here now, right? There should not be secrets between friends, should there?"

Cedric gave a hollow laugh and shook his head. "We terrify you, don't we?"

"The Knights Templar don't terrify me at all. You just alarm me, and probably for good reason. I guess I just didn't think that there would still be people running around rounding up witches. I should have known that things like that would never change, but that makes sense. It just is an unfortunate part of humanity. People seem to always have a burning desire to destroy the unknown. Still, I personally hoped that the days of witch trials were long gone and far behind us."

"Those days could be," Cedric said calmly. "If you and the people like you would just stop practicing your dark magic. It is as simple as that, but you all never seem to stop. I'm not even sure that you are capable of stopping yourselves. The Knights Templar would cease haunting your people down if you gave us actual good reason to retire. But you have not ever done that. We remain active because we need to be. Someone needs to save the world from witchcraft."

"You don't believe that."

"Yes, I do."

"Then why let me live?"

"You seemed like an exception to the rule at the time. Most of the people we purge are the ones that use their magic to hurt other people, and sometimes they do even worse than that. You seemed different for some reason...but now we find that you are teaching someone else, spreading that cursed knowledge to other people. You willingly infect their minds and souls."

"You are upset that I am mentoring someone else and teaching them what I know? Correct me if I'm wrong but wasn't Arthur your mentor in the Knights Templar? He filled your head with all of the bullshit that you try to live by. And I'm sure someday you will help brainwash someone else into the Knights Templar and turn someone else into an executioner. You want to talk about infecting people's minds, look in the mirror or look at any of your Templar pals."

"The Knights Templar did not brainwash me."

"That is what someone who is brainwashed would probably say, don't you think?"

"Whatever the Templar teaches, it is only things that are meant to help the world."

"Is beheading people with those fancy little swords really for the betterment of the earth? What is that really helping?"

"We only execute evil."

"Evil as defined by the Knights Templar. Who are they to decide who is evil and who is not or decide what evil even is? You said it yourself that given their definitions, I was supposed to be purged as part of that evil, but you knew that that was not the case. That was why you spared me. You fought through their creeds that they implanted in your head, or maybe they just didn't do a good enough job getting those thoughts drilled into your head to begin with."

Cedric was trying to keep a brave face on, but Jean could see some cracks forming in his self-assurance. His words might be starting to break through all of the mental armor that the Knights Templar had put on him.

"The point is, you have free will, right? I know you know that because you acted on it before. Just please continue to remember that. I would hate to see a nice kid like you get completely buried by the Knights Templar and all of their outdated beliefs."

For a moment, it looked like he had completely broken through and struck a real chord with Cedric. After a moment, though, the young British man collected himself and crossed his arms.

"I have free will. And I know right from wrong."

Thaddeus butted in awkwardly, hoping to change the subject. "If you two are done already being at each other's throats...don't you think it would be better for us to get more ready for what we could be up against? Between the three of us, I am the one that knows about the vampires. That's obvious. The two of you are like toddlers when it comes to the subject. So how about I enlighten you a little bit?"

The street magician always loved to show off whenever he

could. If he even had a slight edge in some regard over someone else, he was going to point it out and take advantage of it to its absolute fullest. Despite how much more competent Jean and Cedric seemed to be in all other aspects of life, this one thing was enough to completely inflate Thad's ego, and he was going to act like they were complete fools compared to him.

Thaddeus got into it and, given his smug expression, was so happy to have a chance to show them up. Thad made sure to fill them in on all of the "research" that he had done over the years; mostly, that just amounted to having seen far too many movies. It was a crash course history of vampires in pop culture, spanning over one hundred years.

Obviously, the most well-known vampire story was Bram Stoker's novel, *Dracula,* which has been adapted countless times into film, radio shows, TV series, stage plays, and even comic books. In that story, Dracula is said to have been Vlad the Impaler in the back story for his character as he tried to seduce his reincarnated lover. That book and some of its more famous adaptations lay the foundation for so much vampire fiction that came after. The quintessential vampire was widely considered Count Dracula himself, and so many rules were established in that story.

From there, vampire stories covered all kinds of genres of storytelling. Vampires could go from being tragic, romantic figures or mindless bloody monsters depending on the story. Authors like Ann Rice depicted her vampires as beautiful and misunderstood fighting against their bloodlust. Other stories followed suit in one way or another, such as the *Twilight Saga* or *The Vampire Diaries,* where the trades came from immortal romances. Those vampires were trying their best to hold on to their humanity. But that was not always the case.

By contrast, some movies and shows revealed vampires that completely relished their craving for blood. The 1980s spawned two similar vampiric flicks in the same summer with *Near Dark* and *The Lost Boys.* Both of those movies featured gangs of vampires that enjoyed their dark power and used the monsters as allegories for rebellious youth. Thad seemed especially fond of the graphic novel and corresponding movie adaption of the story *30 Days of Night,* where a group of vampires descends on an unsuspecting Alaskan town that does not see the sun for days at a time. It was an interesting concept that ended in an expected bloodbath.There were vampires that were meant to represent cool heroes that people could cheer for, vampires like Blade from Marvel Comics or Selene from *Underworld,* running around firing weapons while wearing flowing black coats.

Some vampires lived in lavish gothic castles, while others lived as next-door neighbors in quaint suburban towns. It all varied. There was no quintessential depiction of a vampire in media, no matter how many appearances they made. Dracula was the archetype, but he certainly was not the only type.

As enlightening as Thaddeus's information about vampires was, it was all about fictional depictions. There was no telling if any of the plethora of things that he was telling them would actually be of any real use in the real world outside of a movie screen. It could all be completely and utterly useless for all they knew, as much as they all hoped that at least something from all of those movies and books and TV shows would actually come in handy. They would eventually find out, and if they did bump into a vampire, hopefully they could channel their inner Van Helsing and slay the beast—but Jean still was not convinced that they would actually find one. Thaddeus Rose's dramatic presentation about the vampires in mass media was not helping him believe that they would actually come across one either. It all just seemed so fake, the more and more that Jean thought about it.

When Thad had finally finished regaling them with all of that information about those monsters, he looked at them like he was expecting them to start clapping their hands and applauding. Neither of them did so, and he looked a bit disappointed by that. Neither of them wanted to feed his ego, especially when there was a good chance that all of his knowledge would be of no real value to them on the upcoming venture.

"Come on, you really are going to pretend like you are not impressed?"

"No need to pretend, man," Jean said. "It's actually a bit concerning that you know that much about vampire stuff. I mean, *Twilight,* really?"

Thad grew a little red but shook his head to try to toss it away. "It's a guilty pleasure...and underrated, honestly. Those books and movies made billions of dollars. They must have been doing something right. And hey, you two aren't fighting anymore, so I did something right for the team."

That was true. That mild, and probably useless, distraction had been enough to calm the tension in the jet and get Jean and Cedric to stop clawing at each other's throats. Jean had never done well with zealots or people that devoted so much of their efforts to a singular cause or religion. People like that just made him uncomfortable because they often were using their faith as a shield to hide behind and make excuses, but that was just a generalization, and he tried not to let that thought influence too much of his opinion. It just made him more cautious around people like that, but those kinds of people also tended to put him on edge.

"So, what can we expect from Romania?" Jean asked. "You've been there before?"

"I have, yes," Cedric said. "The Templar tend to send their knights to all different parts of the world. It helps us understand the cultures around us. We serve the whole world, after all, and not just a singular part of it. It's a good experience and beneficial to be well-traveled. The two of you should try getting out of New Orleans more often. Outside of our fateful trip to the Winchester Mystery House, have you gotten out much?"

"I have, actually," Jean said, though he was lying a little bit. He just did not want to give Cedric any reason to feel superior to them. He didn't need that satisfaction. Between Cedric and Thaddeus, the two other men with Jean were both so full of hot air. "So outside of being one of the Knights Templar's many vacation spots, can you tell us anything about Romania that's actually helpful?"

"Well, one of its most famous historical figures is Vlad the Impaler, obviously. But he lived long ago, though his presence still remains in some regions of the country."

Jean looked at the clouds at the window and thought about what he knew about the infamous Vlad the Impaler. He pulled out one of the books that he had brought on the flight that focused on Vlad himself, knowing that he had connections to vampirism and was from the part of the world they were heading. It was good to be prepared, and he wanted to be ready for what was ahead.

Vlad Tepes was one of the most notorious figures in history. With a nickname like Vlad the Impaler, how could he not be? Jean was not particularly well versed on the topic since he didn't pay much attention to ancient rulers or anything like that unless there was something relating to the supernatural. Vlad's relationship with vampire lore was kind of in a foggy gray area that had never been firmly established, in fact, at least as far as Jean had been aware, but maybe there was more to it than he realized.

Seeing as how Vlad seemed like he was going to be very important to this mystery, Jean did some research online, trying to dig up anything he could about the historical figure. He didn't want to be caught off guard by anything, but if there was any validity to Vlad being a vampire, then maybe the internet would have something to tell him that could be beneficial for their goal.

Jean kept reading, trying to absorb the information as quickly as possible by digesting a whole man's life in the span of about ten minutes. There was simply something depressing about that, that their lives could be summed up like that, but even still, Vlad Tepes accomplished more things than most people did in their lives. He was a force to be reckoned with back then, so of course all kinds of legends would eventually spread.

As much as Jean appreciated learning about unexplained things and the myths that surrounded people, he wanted to make sure that he had a good grasp of who Vlad the man was before deep diving into all of the other bits of stories that may or may not have any sort of validity at all.

Vlad was the ruler of Walachia—a part of what was now modern-day Romania—and was known throughout history as a brutal butcher of a ruler, although despite his reputation, there were historians that argued that he was not nearly as bad as some of the stories or his epithet suggested. Some said he was a fair and just leader whose focus was solely set on protecting and defending his people.

It was hard to really decide which he was, and he imagined that people in that part of the world had differing opinions on him. Nothing in that book said anything about his connections to vampires or Dracula, though. It was purely focused on the historical figure rather than the more mythical aspects to him.

Soon enough, they would be trekking across the same lands that Vlad Tepes once ruled over, and hopefully, they would find the answers for all of the missing blood and the bodies that had once been filled with it. Jean put the book down and just kept watching the clouds until he fell asleep. Hopefully, when he woke up, he would be ready to search for more answers in Vlad the Impaler's homeland.

9

THE LAND OF STAKES

Romania was a very different place than it had been during Vlad the Impaler's times. The landscape wasn't littered with pikes protruding from the ground with human bodies stuck to them for one thing. That made it a much nicer place by default since it was a massive improvement to not have any of that. So much of vampiric lore came from there, especially thanks to the Dracula novel and its use of Transylvania. The place had become synonymous with spooky vampires, dark castles, and full moons, but Jean found a severe lack of all of those things when they arrived in the area. It was actually a very beautiful place.

They were not there to sightsee, though. They had a mission, and it probably wasn't going to bring them anywhere pretty. They needed to follow the trail of that mark and of the ones that it belonged to—the Dracule Bloodline.

"Let's start by searching during the day, yeah?" Thad

suggested. "That way, we remove any advantage if they really are vampires. They'll burn right up if we are outside."

"They're not vampires," Jean said for what felt like the five hundredth time in the past few days. "And besides, if they were vampires, who is to say that any of those stories about sunlight being fatal to them are even true? Maybe nothing would happen."

Thad clicked his tongue and pondered it for a moment. Then he shook his head. "If anything is accurate, it's got to be that. That's like one of the most consistent things in all vampire stories. That and the fangs...and based on the dead bodies...they probably have fangs."

Thaddeus was going to be very disappointed when this cult of Vlad the Impaler worshippers just turned out to be normal crazy people. He had his heart set on real vampires, but that still seemed unlikely to Jean. Given how much he knew about all kinds of supernatural events in the world, he probably would have heard something about vampires being real at some point in time, but he never had. They didn't exist. They couldn't.

The poor people of Romania probably had to deal with all kinds of people asking them about vampires and speaking in atrocious stereotypical Transylvanian accents that Bela Lugosi had made so popular in his tenure as Dracula. The people there must have hated all of that. Their actual history had been tainted by fiction, so now the general public saw them through the lens of fictionalized history rather than actual history. There was something sad about that to Jean. New Orleans was so ingrained by its supernatural history, but at least the majority of those stories had some grains of truth to them; that was a far cry from people coming to Romania expecting to see Dracula's castle. It must have driven Romanians crazy, yet here Jean was—walking with Thad, who was constantly going up to people and asking them about Dracula, being the kind of tourist that Jean was ashamed to even be seen with.

One thing about Thaddeus Rose was that he was not at all afraid of social interaction. He had no fear of going up to people and making a complete fool of himself. One by one, people laughed at his face or shook their heads or asked him to leave. He was not the best at picking up a trail, but realistically, there was probably no real trail to find.

Jean instead focused his efforts away from the vampiric Dracula and instead on the Dracule Bloodline cult. It was much more likely that they were real instead of Dracula miraculously having existed. Given the bodies' drained blood and those symbols, that pack of murderers would be more likely to find than any actual vampires.

They spent a couple of days searching in their respective ways. Neither was very successful, not until luck finally seemed to be in their favor.

Something caught Jean's eye while they were sitting having breakfast at an outside patio. It was a very familiar symbol spray-painted onto the wall of a nearby alley. He could just make it out and instinctively got up from the table and strolled up to it.

"What is it?" Cedric asked, getting up from the table. "I take it, you have found something?"

"Yeah," Jean called back. "I definitely think I found something. For sure. I have no doubt about that."

As he approached, it became clearer and clearer that it was an identical V that had been found on those bodies. Cedric and Thaddeus followed close behind him and caught sight of what he was looking at, and they recognized it immediately too.

"Is that—?"

"It is," Jean said. "The symbol of the Dracule Bloodline."

"So, we are on the right track then?" Thad asked excitedly. They were thrilled to just even have a small crumb to follow.

"It definitely seems like it."

"Can I help you?" A pale bald man stepped out from the shadows of the alley. No one had even noticed him at first, so he must have been very light on his feet. "You looking for something?"

Jean was usually pretty cautious around strangers, but he was especially cautious when those strangers came out of nowhere and seemed inherently suspicious.

"I think we have found what we are looking for, thanks," Jean said, hoping that would be enough to brush the stranger off. It apparently wasn't since the bald man remained.

The stranger smiled at them, and when he did, that grin revealed that his teeth had been filed to sharp points. He looked gleeful as he glanced at the insignia on the building wall and the reaction it was creating in the ones looking at it.

"Ah, I see that you are curious about the Dracule Bloodline."

The stranger's suspiciousness was no longer inherent; it was very blatant. Jean clenched his fist, wanting to be ready for anything. He decided to play dumb.

"We were just admiring the spray paint. What is the Dracule Bloodline?"

The bald man didn't stop flashing his sharp, toothy smile. He obviously saw right through that and shook his head.

"It is no secret," the man said. "Come with me, and I can show you so much more about them. I will tell you everything you want to know."

"Not interested, thanks," Jean said, keeping up the act as long as he could. He had no intention of following a stranger into a dark alleyway. That wasn't a good idea. "We will be getting back to our breakfast."

Jean, Thad, and Cedric turned to leave the alley but found that the entrance had been blocked by a large, imposing man with a matching grin—complete with teeth that had been filed to sharp points. That man had become a wall blocking their escape, and now they were surrounded on both sides.

"You know what, fine." Jean dropped the act. "I guess you are the Dracule cult that have been murdering people and carving that symbol into them. Is that right?"

The bald man giggled and repeated his previous statement. "Follow me, and I will tell you everything that you want to know."

"It does not seem like we have much of a choice," Thad said. "Way to lead us right into a trap, Jean."

It wasn't like he meant to do that. These people had set up a web, and they were just becoming the unfortunate insects that got caught in it. Both Dracule members moved closer, coming at them from both directions of the narrow alleyway. They were closing in quickly.

Cedric reached into his jacket to try to draw his short sword, but the larger Dracula grabbed hold of his arm before he could unsheathe his weapon. Without that sword, they probably didn't stand much of a chance, especially when that big man shoved a cloth over Cedric's mouth and the Templar Knight suddenly went limp and fell to the ground unconscious. They were using chloroform to incapacitate them. They would probably do the same to Jean and Thaddeus.

Jean started to speak the first incantation that came to mind. He didn't know if he really knew any spell work that could actually help in this particular situation, but he was going to give it a try. Unfortunately, few sounds left his mouth before the bald stranger pulled out his own rag of chloroform and forced it over Jean's mouth, silencing him.

As he started to fall into unconsciousness, Jean just worried about what he would wake up to. He wanted to find this cult of murderers, but he did not want to find them under these kinds of circumstances. Being a prisoner was not the most ideal way to learn more about them. It was probably just a matter of time before he became another one of their victims with a V carved into his flesh.

INTERLUDE - THE MAN WHO WANTED TO LIVE FOREVER

Mikael had always been fascinated by the prospect of living forever. That would be a completely different experience compared to the limited time that most people had on their own mortal coils. Just imagining what could be done with all of the time in the world made him so excited about the possibility, no matter how impossible it seemed. If someone had forever to live, they could experience everything and see everything. That sounded unbelievable.

That was why vampires always captivated him so much. He wanted to understand how it felt to be like that, even if he had to give up his humanity to do it. Unfortunately, he initially believed that vampires were just works of fiction but living in Romania, the notion of vampirism was practically ingrained in some of the darker parts of their culture.

It seemed to trace back to Vlad the Impaler, who had connections to vampiric legends thanks to his inclusion in the Dracula novel and to old stories about his brutality. He was a hero to some, but it was those darker fables about him that captured Mikael's attention and the more he learned about him, the more he became fascinated by the idea that Vlad might have discovered the secret to eternal life.

Mikael knew all too well how short life could be. Human beings only had a century to be part of the world, and in the grand scheme of things, that was not an ideal time at all. Few people even made it close to actually living that long anyway. Both of Mikael's parents died when he was just a boy and when they were still relatively young. His father died during an armed robbery, and his mother shortly after of an illness. Losing them both like that showed him how fleeting life was and just how fragile human beings really were. Millions of things could kill them at any moment, and no matter how carefully someone lived this life, time would eventually catch up with them no matter what.

Mikael hated thinking about his mortality. Just the thought of dying and no longer being in the world would make his heart start pounding in his chest and make sweat pour out all over his body. It would even make it hard for him to sleep and the looming and ever-present threat of death weighed down on him at every waking moment. He could not escape that feeling of dread no matter how hard he tried to get away from it.

He tried all kinds of methods to ease his mind and find some comfort, but nothing worked. Mikael's mind races too much for meditation to give him any peace, so that was not effective. Taking pills for his anxiety and to help him fall asleep did not do much either. They apparently weren't strong enough to work on all of the horrors his unconscious mind conjured of his doom.

Religion was what a lot of other people turned to since they found comfort in the notion that there was some sort of afterlife waiting for them beyond their mortal coil, but Mikael was never much of a believer in those kinds of things. So many religions acted like the world was a neat and tidy place, but it was never as simple as they liked to pretend that it was. Heaven and Hell did not even sound like ideal ways to spend eternity after death either; Hell was obviously meant to sound awful, but even Heaven was not somewhere that Mikael wanted to go since a perfect paradise where everyone was happy lacked all of the complexities of the world. The mortal world was imperfect and sometimes awful, but at least it was real. No, he found no solace in the afterlives that religions talked about.

Mikael even tried counseling and therapy, but the people he spoke with just talked endlessly about focusing on the positives and on the bright sides of life. That all sounded good in principle, but Mikael knew that even the brightest things to latch on to in life would eventually dim just like the sun itself would one day flicker out and die. It was a depressing thought, but it was the truth. The psychologists that he spoke to diagnosed him as being someone suffering from thanatophobia, which they described as anxiety and fear of your own death. That seemed accurate and made sense when he heard it, but just because it was categorized didn't mean that his crippling worry just went away; it actually made it worse to talk about it since it made it even more real. His whole life seemed like a depressing wait to be buried in the earth to rot and be forgotten—it was just not fair.

Driven by his own terror that he could not get rid of, Mikael started researching ways to prolong life. He wanted to find anything that would keep him alive as long as possible, to stay away from that inevitable void waiting to claim him at the end of his days. There were obvious answers; making sure to exercise regularly, trying to eat healthily, and avoiding bad habits like smoking, but all of those were just drivel that would not actually do him much good. The healthiest people on the planet still did not usually live over a hundred years.

It just was not right for humans to have such a short life span. They could only exist for the briefest second of time in an indifferent universe. There had to be something, some way to avoid the maws of death, and he made it his life's goal to find it.

There were all kinds of legends about things that could grant someone immortality, but there was no real evidence of any truth to any of those things. The Fountain of Youth was probably just a soothing hot spring that helped relieve muscles. The Holy Grail was probably just some cup that no one had sipped from in thousands of years. All of those legends were just legends, but there was some closer to home that caught his eye, and it came back to the interest in vampires that he always had.

It was a symbol that grabbed his attention, a simple V that he had seen in all kinds of places. He had never really paid much attention to that symbol before, but when he really looked into what it meant, he found more than he bargained for—and almost exactly what he was looking for.

The symbol belonged to a group known as the Dracule Bloodline, and they had been operating in Mikael's homeland of Romania for hundreds of years, dating all the way back to the times of Vlad the Impaler, when the country was part of Walachia. They were apparently made up of servants, retainers, and vassals for Vlad Tepes, that all knew his darkest secrets. The whole world associated Vlad with vampires thanks to the Dracula story, but after learning all about the Dracule Bloodline, it was starting to sound like Vlad's history with vampiric lore was more than just artistic literary liberty. There was maybe something more concrete to it all.

Mikael started digging more into the Dracule Bloodline even though there was not much solid information about them. Most of the information came from Internet forums and message boards where people discussed the strange V symbol that appeared in all kinds of places across Romania. There were all kinds of speculations ranging from it being a call to arms for an underground political anarchist moment to some kind of criminal gang symbol. Some even thought that it was some kids defacing properties with their own symbol just for fun. No one knew for certain what the cause was except for the strange posts from people claiming to be part of the Dracule Bloodline. Their posts proclaimed that they were looking for new members and that the people that joined them would gain eternal life since the Dracule were supposedly close to attaining immortality. Mikael was not exactly sure what they meant by that, but it captured his curiosity anyway.

Mikael followed their postings online and sent them an email inquiring for more information. He waited anxiously for a response, praying that he would hear back. Of all of the ways that he had tried to find something useful, this one seemed like it had the most potential to actually lead somewhere. For all he knew, it could be a waste of time, but he had a good feeling about it—they just needed to get back to him. After many more hours of waiting by his computer, he finally got a response.

It was a simple line of text, and all that it stated was a location, a meeting place where they wanted to introduce themselves and see if he was fit for a position among them. Mikael hurried to that location that same night, not wanting to waste another second when immortality might be on the line. It was late, and most of the rest of the country was asleep, and when he got there, he found a group of odd-looking people waiting for him. They were all pale and pasty-looking, like they had not seen the sun in months. They all looked at him with mild curiosity.

"Are you...are you the Dracule?" Mikael was almost breathless, completely enraptured by them and by how close he felt to the immortality that he wanted. These people might be his best chance of finding a way to live forever.

One of them, a tall and broad-shouldered man with a beard, stepped forward, and when he spoke, he showed strange sharpened teeth in his mouth that came over his bottom lip at sharp points.

"You were looking to join the Dracule?"

Mikael felt a small tingle of hesitation at the sight of that man's teeth but nodded. He knew that this was exactly where he needed to be if he wanted to make his dreams a reality. Somehow it felt like this was the right place to find everlasting life.

"Yes, I would like to join the Dracule."

The man grinned and showed his mouth of pointed teeth again. "And what is it exactly that you hope to gain by joining us?"

Mikael was upfront and honest about his intentions. There was no reason not to be. "I don't want to die. I never want to. So, you are all looking for immortality...I want that too..."

"That is good," the bearded man said. "Because we can show you how to get it. We are close, yes, so close now."

Mikael asked the question that had been on his mind since he first learned about the Dracule Bloodline, and especially after he saw that man's teeth.

"Are you all vampires...?"

The members of the Dracule laughed, and he saw that they all shared those sharp teeth in their mouths.

"No. Not yet, but we are preparing ourselves for when we are."

"What do you mean?" Mikael asked, trying to make sense of what he was hearing. "You are going to somehow become vampires then?"

"We are, yes. Our lord will turn us, and when he does, we will join him in eternity."

Mikael had a guess of who their lord was. Everything that

he had read about the Dracule Bloodline made it obvious who they were referring to. "Your lord...you mean Vlad Tepes."

"Yes."

"So are you saying that he was a vampire then?"

"He is." The present tense was strange and stuck out.

"So, you are saying that he *is* still alive then?"

"Yes and no." That didn't make things much clearer. "He is out there, and when we find him, he will reward us by sharing the gift of immortality."

Mikael was not entirely sure about the plan. It sounded like it was something that was just implausible, but even the possibility of there being a chance of achieving actual immortality was enough to overrule any doubts that he had.

"We will do whatever it takes to find immortality," the Dracule said. "Would you be willing to do anything to find it as well?"

Mikael considered that for a moment. He had been crippled his whole life by his fear of death looming and growing closer each and every minute of each and every day. He would only be able to start living once that constant threat was no longer waiting, when death was no longer a worry. He could finally enjoy life then.

"Yes, I will do whatever it takes."

It probably was not easy for the Dracule Bloodline to find like-minded individuals to recruit, but Mikael fit right in. He dove headfirst into the group, helping them however he could. He had his teeth sharpened and even had chances to read all of the scrolls that the Dracule from centuries ago had left behind.

Some of those old parchments included firsthand accounts of Vlad Tepes and his dark secrets. According to those old comments, the king of Walachia did not age and could not be felled by any weapon that enemies used against him. There were also plenty of parts of the scrolls that discussed Vlad's craving for blood—and it seemed to be the only thing that could satiate him and quench his thirst. The Dracule at the time noticed how much stronger their king would become after having his fill and recognized the blood as the source of his power.

The Dracule never planned for what would happen if their monstrous leader was defeated. They never thought that they would ever have to concern themselves with that possibility since he could not be killed and would live forever. They expected an eternity of greatness under Vlad's rule, never-ending prosperity where their enemies would be put on stakes to suffer and accept their defeat. That was not meant to be, though. Instead, Vlad was apparently slain on the battlefield, impaled by one of the giant stakes that he was so famous for using.

An immortal dying didn't seem possible, but for him, unlike mortals, it was a temporary death. Vlad could be resuscitated if given enough blood. The problem was that no one, not even his loyal Dracule, knew where Vlad's body had ended up. That made it very difficult to bring him back, but if they could do it, then he might be so grateful that he would make them like him. The chance of that was so exciting for Mikael. He wanted that more than he had ever wanted anything before in his life.

Months with the Dracule turned to years, and he worked tirelessly to try to track down what had happened to Vlad's remains, scouring the globe for anything that could help find them. It was not an easy task, and for him, every second meant aging just a little bit more and more, growing ever closer to the end of his own life. He needed to hurry and permanently extend his life before there was no life to make eternal anyway.

Some of his fellow Dracule were not so fortunate, and their time on the mortal plane came to an end before they ever even had the chance to get the immortality that they spent their life trying to attain. The bearded man that recruited Mikael to begin with, Pietro, died within the first couple of years after that fateful meeting; he would never get to enjoy the fruits of the Dracules' collective labor. Mikael did not want the same thing to happen to him. He wanted to—no, needed to—find Vlad's remains and revive him.

But as time went on, it seemed less and less likely. Mikael could feel time ticking away and his life evaporating right before his eyes. He was growing older, and he needed to find immortality before he completely expired.

Finally, after centuries of searching the globe, they finally found something. It was in Romania, right under their nose, the most likely location of the remains. They would be left there for now until they collected the blood that they needed to revive their lord. The Dracule Bloodline had kept the ancient resuscitation ritual to bring Vlad back from his death and to restore his power. All it required was blood—a great deal of blood.

Mikael knew immortality was close now. He just needed to gather the proper materials. The blood that he would need and the lives that he would take to get it would simply be a necessary sacrifice. Those lives would be used to extend his own, and he would put those years to much better use than those people ever could.

10

IMPRISONED FAR FROM THE SUN

Jean woke up to a throbbing head and inside of a room that was almost pitch black. He was laying on his back, and when he sat up, he realized that the reason the room was so dark was that all of the windows had been boarded up. Small slivers of sunlight could be seen but could not break through the planks of wood. The whole room was shrouded except for one singular light bulb that flickered on and off in the corner.

A pale man with dirty-blonde hair sat on a stool beneath that light bulb, and he watched Jean sit up with a great deal of interest.

"Good morning," the man said, in a heavy Eastern European accent. "It looks like you had a rough night."

Jean stretched his arms and slowly got to his feet. "It could have been better probably, but I've had worse. You wouldn't believe some of the places where I woke up in the morning after a crazy night. I'm not ashamed to admit that.

That being said, this might be the strangest place that I have ever woken up in. What's with the windows?"

"They keep out the sunlight, of course."

Jean chuckled a little and rolled his eyes. "You are really milking this vampire thing, aren't you? You think kidnapping me is going to convince me that you are the real deal? Maybe turn into a bat, and then maybe I will change my tune."

"I don't really care what you believe," the man said. "I would just like to know what you and your friends are doing here. And why is it that you are looking for us?"

"Why do you think?" Jean said with a little laugh. "Start killing people, draining all of their blood from their bodies, and carving some symbols on their bodies...that is going to raise more than a few eyebrows, you idiot. If you were trying to keep a low profile, that's not how you do it."

"I'm just impressed that you managed to track us down."

"It wasn't hard. That's what leaving a trail of weird bodies in your wake will do. So, you are part of that cult then? The one that the symbol you have been tagging people with comes from, right? What was it called again...?"

"The Dracule Bloodline."

"Yes, that. Very cryptic. Very scary. So give it to me straight... Are you people vampires or not?"

"And if I told you that we are?"

"Then I probably wouldn't believe you. But again, there are other ways that you can prove yourself. For one thing, pull one of those planks off of the window and let's see if you burn in the sun. How does that sound? To me, that sounds perfect."

"That is not going to happen."

"So, from what I know about Dracule Bloodline, you people are absolutely obsessed with Vlad the Impaler, right? So, what exactly is it that draws you to him so much? Where does that deep love come from? Do you just love the way that he would skewer people with giant pikes, or are you more partial to his actual geographical conquests? Whatever the case, I feel like there are more moral people that you could fawn over instead of devoting your life to a seven-hundred-year-old maniacal tyrant. It just seems a bit desperate, doesn't it? Like you are just looking for a purpose anywhere you can."

His captor glowered at him. "Don't pretend like you know anything about us. Just because you managed to find us does not mean that you actually know anything. You don't."

"You're right. I don't. So, let's get to know each other better, how about that? My name is Jean, and I have always had a fascination with the occult, but luckily, I have never had a fascination with a cult...unlike you. You seem to have sold yourself wholesale to this Dracule gang."

"My name is Mikael," the man growled. "And that cult that you are speaking of is my life's work. And I am not just a member. I am its current leader."

"Great," Jean said. That made things easier. He would rather talk to someone that knew what they were talking about than some grunt who didn't know anything useful. "So, you and your boys have been running around and squeezing blood out of all kinds of people...for what, exactly?"

"That is none of your concern. It has nothing to do with you, Jean. Although, it will have a little bit to do with you soon. When we take your blood, then you will in some way become part of all of this. But for now, and until then, do not worry about it."

"It's going to be hard not to worry about it when apparently I'm one of the next victims. It doesn't exactly ease my mind to know that I am on the list to get bled out."

"Well, you would never have been if you did not meddle in things that did not concern you. Our mission is one that we do not like to tell people about. We have kept to ourselves. The Dracules have barely been more than whispers for centuries. We were careful, we were quiet, and we avoided situations like this. But now, now we have to adapt and change some of our ways because of you and your friends. Do you know how irritating that is?"

"I can only imagine," Jean said. "It's probably as irritating as listening to you threatening to take my blood and then not tell me anything more than that. Oh wait, you also mentioned that this is an unmitigated disaster for your cult, and you are the one that's supposed to be in charge. That must be embarrassing. You could at least confirm to me if you are a vampire or not. That would at least be something."

"What would you like me to say? That I am hundreds of

years old and that I feed on blood and can be killed by a stake to the heart? Perhaps you would like me to say that I hate the taste of garlic. Would that satisfy your curiosity?"

"A simple yes or no would probably do the trick, to be honest."

"No then. Does that suffice? I am not a vampire, but we are preparing for the time when we may be."

That sounded like absolute lunacy that Jean planned to call out, but he didn't get the chance as Mikael continued to speak.

"We in the Dracule Bloodline are just simple human beings, mortals dedicated to a united cause. We have been devoted to serving Vlad Tepes for centuries, since its lifetime. We served him well then, abiding by his every command. The members of the Dracule then kept many records about their master and his odd habits. They knew exactly what he was. They brought people to him—peasants, servants, other noblemen, whoever he wanted to satiate his hunger. They knew who they were serving. They saw his power and that it was like no other power in the world. They wanted it, and he was going to share it with them."

"What do you mean share it with them? He was going to turn them? Make more vampires?"

"Yes, yes. He would feed them his blood and sire them. Best of all, his everlasting life would be theirs as well. Imagine that. Immortality. That is truly what they all wanted. The atrocities that our lord committed against humanity could be overlooked if it meant attaining an eternal life. After all, how could we judge an immortal for mortal crimes? He should not have been held to the same standards as most men."

Jean wasn't so sure about that. Just because Vlad might have been a monster did not mean that he was allowed to just slaughter people. It sounded like the Dracule or whatever just didn't care about the lives of other people if they had a chance of improving their own lives. That was how it really seemed to him. Anything else was just an excuse.

"After our master fell, the Dracule knew that he could potentially be brought back and that a vampire's death may be temporary. With enough blood, his strength could be restored. However, most of the Dracule were wiped out by Vlad's enemy, and it took many generations for us to rebuild to a place where we could continue our work, when we could actually start to attempt to restore him."

The Dracule sounded like they had been on the verge of extinction. It probably would have been better if a group like that had actually been destroyed for good. That probably would have been better for the world in the long run, considering they were now trying to bring some ancient beast back.

"Vlad Tepes's body was never found, his remains hidden from the world. That was because of us. The Dracule hid him away, hoping that as a vampire, he was not dead for good. According to the early writers of the Dracule that were around at the time of his death, giving Vlad enough blood will restore him to his former glory."

"What happened to him? How did he even die the first time?"

"He was defeated on the battlefield in the middle of the day when the sun was at its highest. From there, he was impaled by one of his own wooden pikes as punishment for what he had put others through. In a way, he had been staked through the heart in that moment, and that had ended his life. But he would not remain so...not if he could be revived. His followers, our ancestors, waited for the chance to revive him. But to come back from that state, he needed a great deal of blood. He was entombed, buried deep within the earth, where the sun could not reach him. From there, we just needed to collect enough blood to perform a ritual that could restore him."

Jean nodded. "I have read about the power of blood. And I'm well aware how many kinds of magic utilized it for some very powerful witchcraft."

"Yes," Mikael said. "Blood is life force, what fuels a body and allows it to work. The ritual we prepare to use was created by the Dracule over centuries, aided by witches and warlocks to ensure that it would work. We had to be careful due to how powerful that kind of magic can be."

"But for something like that, a blood ritual of that size, you would need a lot of blood. More than just a few bodies' worth."

Mikael smirked with some pride. "We have been even busier than you have been led to believe. Only some of our work has gotten noticed, but much of it has been done with complete anonymity. Follow me."

They walked through that dark building, where only dim lamps provided any real light to see. Mikael unlocked a heavy-looking door and pushed it open. A blast of cold air spilled out, revealing that it was some kind of freezer. Inside, there were rows of metal barrels lined up along the walls. There were dozens upon dozens of barrels stored inside.

Jean almost couldn't believe his own eyes. His gut instinct immediately told him what was most likely contained inside of those barrels, but it was impossible to be able to see anything inside of them to confirm his suspicions. The only way to know was to ask.

"What is inside of those barrels?" Jean asked, already having his own guess and was fairly certain that he knew the answer already. Still, he wanted to know for sure.

"Those?" Mikael smirked. "Those are the result of all of the hard work that we have been doing to fulfill our purpose."

"And by that, you mean blood, right? It's blood." Jean wanted to dispense with a lot of vague suspense and nonanswers. "The blood that you took from your victims when you people killed them. It's not just evidence of your dedication to this messed-up cult of yours. This is evidence of murder."

"Call it what you wish. It was all a necessary sacrifice."

"More like the deluded crimes of a group of lunatics."

"I thought that you would be more understanding. You are an occult expert after all."

"I don't think any width of an open mind would make up

for what you people have done. There is belief, and then there is insanity. Doing this...taking all of this blood like this...this is the latter. There is no doubt about that in my mind."

"Perhaps if you got a better look at our accomplishments..."

Mikael pushed him closer to the barrels and unscrewed the top of one of them, prying it open. Sure enough, inside was a pool of dark red liquid—the blood that Jean expected to find. He didn't expect Mikael to dip a finger into it and lick it up off of his digit, though. That was a bit disgusting. He was really leaning into this whole vampire thing.

"Blood is the source of life," Mikael said, giving credence to what Jean had already been musing about. "That is how vampires sustain their eternal lives. That is where their power comes from. The power of others becomes their own. And it is the power that we will use to bring him back. And it is the power that we will consume once our lord gifts us with immortality. Some people think of the act of drinking another's blood as being some evil act, but it is not evil. It is survival. All sentient creatures understand survival."

"You seem to have this all well planned out, man, but what happens if this doesn't work? Then you collected all of that blood and killed all of those people for nothing?"

Mikael shrugged. "That is unfortunately the cost of attempting something that has never been done before. But the chance of failure should not be enough to deter one from going down that path as they will never know the real answers until they reach the end."

"The ends justify the means and all of that bullshit then? Cool. Glad to know that you have no empathy for other people at all."

"Other people don't really concern me," Mikael said with a disturbing amount of calm. "They are temporary. Why bother concerning myself with others when they will be dead before long? Even the longest I would have to put up with someone might be a century but usually never even that. And once I have my immortality, then those people will mean even less to me. Their existence would just be a blip in my never-ending life. Their mortal problems would be trivial."

The longer they spoke, the more and more delusional the leader of the Dracule Bloodline seemed to really be. It was more than a little concerning that their fates were in the hands of people like him. He might kill them on a whim and take all of their blood, just to try to appease Vlad the Impaler, who had been dead for half a millennium.

"Well, my mortal problem right now, man, is that I am being held captive with my friends. I know it may seem...trivial, like you said...but it's actually kind of a major problem right now, and I'm not a big fan of it. We came here trying to find the source of all of those bodies and those symbols, and now we have, so can't we just be on our way now that I've got my answers?"

Mikael laughed. "If only it were that easy, yes? It's not. If we let you go now, then you will go inform the authorities of what is going on, and we will be arrested for all of those sacrifices that we enacted. We will be brought down by people that could never comprehend the gravity of what we are doing here. So, no, you and your traveling companions will remain right where you were. I am actually going to speak to them next."

Without another word, Mikael turned and let them the room, locking the door behind him. Jean was back to being alone again and dreaded the conversations that a psycho cultist like him was going to have with Cedric and Thad. He and Cedric might be able to bond about both blindly following their cults, but he couldn't even begin to fathom what he was going to talk to Thaddeus about.

"I would like my sword back."

Cedric McKellan didn't expect to be taken prisoner on this assignment, but so far, his track record with the Knights Templar had not been the best. He had catastrophically failed his first assignment, getting one of his comrades killed and sparing the life of someone that should have been an enemy. This second assignment was not faring much better. He was supposed to be getting answers and stopping the killings. He might get some answers, but it seemed like he would just be yet another one in the series of murders. He wondered what part of his body would be where they would carve that symbol that they loved so much.

The leader of the Dracule Bloodline waved the gleaming

sword in front of him, obviously trying to taunt him. "No. I do not think that it would be a smart move to give my prisoner his weapon back. That sounds like an easy way to get myself killed, and I like living. I like it a lot."

"What are you worried about? It's not like my sword would be able to do anything to an immortal monster like you, eh? So, you have nothing to fear."

Mikael let out a loud bellow of laughter. "What is it with you people? You all just assume that I am a vampire without much evidence of such."

"I don't actually believe it," Cedric said. He really didn't, but he figured he would humor the notion given the boarded-up windows that were keeping the sun from shining into the room. "But it is nice to know that that probably is not the case. That makes my job here much easier if I don't have to become a vampire slayer."

"Your job?"

"Yes, my job. I was investigating those murders you and your cult committed to see if there was anything supernatural about them. The prevailing theory was that you were real-life vampires. But, I highly doubted that. I have seen some things that science could never explain, but vampires seemed far-fetched."

"They are not far-fetched. I am just not one of them. But there was one man who was. Vlad Tepes, better known as Vlad the Impaler."

Cedric thought—or maybe hoped—that he misheard him for a moment. It sure sounded like this man really believed in vampires. Not only that, but he was part of a cult that worshipped the historical figure that he now claimed was a vampire. If they really believed that Vlad was a real-life Dracula, then it was no wonder that a creepy, misguided blood worshipping cult had formed in honor of him.

"You think Vlad the Impaler was an actual vampire?"

"We know he was," Mikael said. "And most of the world does too. They just write it off as being a fun...what do you call it...ah, yes, a fun quirk. They like to play with the idea that *Bram Stoker's Dracula* novel was just conjecture and his connection with Vlad the Impaler was just a little piece of trivia and not based on any fact. But it was fact. Vlad Tepes was an immortal being and perhaps even the progenitor of the vampire species. There are so many stories about it in plain sight, but no one actually takes it seriously—no one but us. We see what it is. We know it as the truth."

"How do you know that?"

"The Dracules have served Vlad since the days that he was walking the earth. They kept a great many private records about him and his life. Within those records is the truth of what kind of ruler that Vlad Tepes really was and the truth about what kind of man he was as well. They talk about how he was not a man at all but a creature wearing the skin of a mortal man, a creature that needed to drink the blood of the living in order to survive."

"So, you are going to trust some old writings and base all of your beliefs on some old parchments?"

"Correct me if I am wrong, Cedric, but you and the Knights Templar read the Bible, do you not? A text from millennia ago that you read and follow, swearing to live your lives based on the words contained on those pages. How is that any different from taking our own beliefs from the words of ones that came before us? You have your God, and I have mine."

Mikael pointed Cedric's own sword at him.

"When this is over, we will have taken the blood from your body and collected it just like we have with all of our victims."

"But why?" Cedric asked. "What's the point of taking everyone's blood? Is it just to keep up this whole vampire motif? That seems a bit extreme just to keep up your performance, eh?"

"We take the blood for a much more specific and useful purpose. It is not just for show. Rest assured." Mikael placed the tip of the blade up against Cedric's neck, and the tip of it pressed down and drew blood. "What is inside of you will soon be outside of you, harvested for our own purposes. But do not worry. Your blood will be used to help change this world."

Thaddeus had already wound up in so many dangerous situations since he met Jean-Luc Gerard. As terrified as he was, he always wanted his life to have more excitement; he really should have been more careful with what he wished for. There was a difference between wanting adventure and actually experiencing one. The dangers in stories were thrilling and enjoyable but actually being put into those situations was a different story altogether. He had quickly realized how much worse that was. Being taken as a prisoner of some cult in Romania was not exactly something he ever wanted to experience. He had far too many plans for his future to have it cut short by people like that. As much as he was enjoying learning from Jean, it might not be worth it if he ended up dead before he got to accomplish all of his career goals.

The door to the room he had been locked in suddenly opened, and a new person walked in. Thad recognized authority when he saw it, and this guy carried himself with a lot of it.

"Hello, my name is Mikael," the man said with a friendly tone. "From what I have heard, you are some kind of wizard?"

"Magician," Thaddeus said, a bit surprised but also glad that his reputation apparently preceded him. "But I will take wizard too, absolutely. So what else have you heard about me?"

"Just that," Mikael said. "I have spoken with the two men that you were traveling with. From what I have gathered, they do not seem to appreciate your talents. They see you as expendable, and they themselves are uncooperative. That is fairly common. There are so many underappreciated people in this world. But we appreciate outcasts and the ones that are misunderstood. So many people like that have found a place with us."

Thaddeus laughed a little bit. "Are you trying to recruit me right now?"

"And if I am?"

"Well, you would have to go through my handler for that. I could have you get in touch with her, and from there, we could work out a contract and iron out any appearances that I will be making. Until that happens, well...I'm afraid I can't make any real commitments to any other gigs. What might make me more interested in the idea is if you let me and my friends go for one thing. As a show of good faith?"

"That is not going to happen, but I understand your desire for all of this tension to settle. I tried to do as much myself. I tried to convince your friends that we don't have to be enemies, but it is just as I said, they are being very uncooperative. But you seem more sensible than them."

"What if I join this cult—I mean, group—of yours? What then? Would you let them go if I did that?"

"Of course not," Mikael said bluntly. "They know far too much about us for that. The Dracule Bloodline has survived for centuries by remaining in the shadows and away from the sun, keeping out of sight from any prying eyes. You and your friends...you have prying eyes. That is a problem for us as I am sure you can understand. It impedes everything that we are trying to do. We are not at our full strength when we cannot operate quietly and unseen. You shine a light upon us. All of our power is gone."

"Like a vampire..." Thad mused with a sad little laugh. "That's what this whole group of yours is about, right? I get it. I love vampires. I probably know more about them than every member of your cult combined."

"I doubt that," Mikael said but looked intrigued. "Still, it is good to hear that vampirism is an interest of yours. That makes you an even better candidate to join us. Haven't you ever thought about what it would be like to be a vampire? Haven't you ever wanted to be turned and get to experience that kind of life? Haven't you ever wanted immortality?"

Mikael was surprisingly good at pitching his crazy ideas. Some of it almost sounded very appealing to Thaddeus. Of course, he had wanted to understand what it felt like to be a vampire. That was part of the appeal of vampires in fiction. You could vicariously see what it was like to live forever, giving in to your darkest urges.

"Immorality would be something, yeah," Thad said. "But I don't think I need to be turned into a vampire to get that. I have already charted my course to make sure that I can live forever through the minds and memories of other people. I will make sure that I am never forgotten and that my name echoes through the lifetimes in the minds of human beings. That's good enough for me."

"Is it?" Mikael shook his head. "That sounds lovely, but fame and fortune is nothing compared to actual eternal life. You want to spend a lifetime carving your name into the history books, but just imagine how much more you could do if you had multiple lifetimes to do it. Does that not sound so much better than what you are hoping for?"

Once again, he was being very convincing.

"You are acting like it's an actual option."

"It is," Mikael said.

"How? By drinking the blood that you took from all of those people?"

"We will not drink it, no," Mikael said. "We ourselves are not yet vampires, but soon enough, we may be. If we continue to pursue this to the very end, then we will be rewarded with everlasting life. Immortality is within our grasp. We are so very close now. And we can't let you people get in the way of that. The Dracule Bloodline will not allow that."

"How are you going to get immortality then?"

"The same way most vampires do," Mikael said simply, like that was supposed to make sense. "We will have to be turned."

"Be turned...right..." Thaddeus shook his head. "But wouldn't that require another vampire to turn you?"

"It would," Mikael said and smiled, showing off his own sharp teeth. "What do you think we are gathering blood for?"

Thaddeus wracked his brain as his mind bounced wildly between ideas. None of this made sense, but everything he knew about vampires was starting to add up. These people must have been gathering blood for some vampire to drink, but vampires should not have actually been real. All of this was insane. All of these cultists planned on gaining immortality and apparently had a vampire lined up to help give it to them.

Thad had to keep playing along, try to glean any more information off of Mikael that he could. "Alright then. You have my interest. So, what do I have to do to become a full-blown member of the Dracule? Do we start with sharpening my teeth?"

Mikael snickered, but there was no actual humor in his voice. "I am afraid that we have moved past that opportunity. At least for now. This conversation has shown me that you are too loyal to your friends already. Even if you did join us right now, we would not be able to trust you."

Thad wished he had not stuck his foot in his mouth so soon into this talk. He should have been more careful with how he spoke to this stranger. He should have played along more. Instead, his cover was blown before he even had a chance to try to go undercover. The one thing he could have done to help them get out of this situation was already ruined.

"Maybe sometime in the future, once we have embraced our new lives, we may be inclined to give you our new gifts, but for now...you are one of them. But you will see. You will see that we are not as crazy as you believe."

Thaddeus doubted that. He had a great deal of passion for vampiric lore, but he would always recognize the absolute insanity of these vampire worshippers.

"So, tell me this then... Do you and your friends here really believe that you are vampires? Like actual real-life vampires? I see the teeth and all of that, but I can't imagine that you actually believe that that is true."

Mikael gave a little smile but did not immediately answer. He had to give it some thought, and that in itself was an answer. If he had to consider it that much, then he definitely thought that he was really a vampire.

"I mean, the teeth that you all have given yourselves were kind of a dead giveaway that you had taken this delusion of yours to the furthest extreme possible. I'm not really judging, though. I'm not. Really. It's just all really fascinating. I would love to get my camera crew over here, and we could do a whole documentary on the Dracule Bloodline. Who knows, maybe that will help spread the word for your vampire deity."

"Enough," Mikael said venomously. "You do not know when to stop talking, do you?"

Before long, the Dracules had tossed Thaddeus into the room with Jean. He looked a little bruised and battered, but overall, he was in one piece. He tried to shake whatever injuries he had off. When he finally seemed to get his balance, he coughed out a little chuckle.

"I don't think that they are real vampires."

"You don't say," Jean said. "What was your first clue?"

"Well, they have not fed on me. At least not yet. I have to say, I am a little bit disappointed if they are not. Them being vampires would be so much more fun than them just being a bunch of nutjobs obsessed with vampires. It's not even close."

"What did they ask you?"

"All kinds of things, but I think they got annoyed by me after a little while." That sounded about right. "I probably ended up asking them more questions than they asked me. I went through the checklist of all of the signs that someone was a vampire, seeing if they matched all of the criteria. I can tell you right now that they probably only reached about a thirty percent match. I told them as much too. I guess they didn't think that I was worth killing either, which I honestly find a little bit insulting..."

"They might just be waiting to kill you for later. It sounds like that is what they are going to do with me. They are going to drain my blood and use it for something. They didn't say for what."

"If they were vampires, I would say that maybe they are going to mix your blood with cocktails or something or use it as a condiment for their food or something. But since, as it turns out, they are not vampires—I don't have a clue." Thad patted down his pants and then let out a groan. "They took my phone, so it looks like we're very, very stuck here."

"Who would you even have called? Dani and Kaleb?"

"Maybe. So? Dani is my handler. She should know where I am."

"They are in a completely different part of the world. What help do you think that would be? Besides, if you get the chance to make a call for rescue, try calling the actual authorities."

"I wouldn't even know where to tell them to go, though," Thad said defeatedly.

That was true. With how the windows had been completely blocked out, it was hard to even gauge what time it was outside because it seemed like they were just enshrouded in complete and utter darkness indefinitely. Jean really hoped that they would get out of there. He really missed the outside world already. He did not want that dank and dark room to be his tomb.

The door opened, and suddenly, Cedric McKellan was thrown in to join them. He looked very angry and a far cry from the professionally dressed collected individual that he liked to present himself as—or maybe that the Knights Templar required him to appear as. He tried to get back to the door before they closed it, but it was too late, and they heard the lock turn.

"These bastards really think that they can just get away with doing this to us? Seriously? They even took my sword. I really need that back."

"Forget about the sword," Thaddeus hissed. "It wasn't even all that great anyway. And can't your rich Templar friends just make you a new one?"

"It's not that simple!" Cedric snapped. "A knight's sword is everything to them. Once they are given to us, they become a part of us. They become an extension of your soul and your intent and a tool to carry out the Templar's goals. Being awarded one only happens when you are fully inducted into the Knights Templar, so it is far more profound than I think any of you understand. It represents all of the work it took to get to that point, an award for becoming a true warrior of God."

"Oh, please," Thaddeus scoffed. "It is really just a nice piece of metal with an okay ruby on the hilt of it. You don't have to be so dramatic about it."

It was weird to hear Thad tell someone else not to be so dramatic. Usually, Thaddeus was the absolute drama queen, at least as long as Jean had known him.

"We can't focus on that right now," Jean said. "We need to figure out how to get the hell away from these people. This whole cult of theirs is insane."

"You don't say," Cedric said. "Really, eh? I hadn't noticed. What gave it away? The fact that they are murdering people and stealing their blood or that they blacked out all of their windows so no sunlight could get in?"

"Yeah, what is up with that?" Thad said. The street magician paused, and it seemed like a light bulb went off in his head. "Renfield."

"What?"

"Renfield," Thaddeus said again, as if just repeating that word would somehow make more sense than the first time he said it. It didn't. He looked like Sherlock Holmes at the end of a complicated case, like he had solved some puzzle that no one else had been able to. "Renfield. You know Renfield, right?"

Jean and Cedric shook their heads together. Jean did not have a clue what Thad was even talking about. Whatever Renfield was sounded familiar, but he definitely didn't know what it was really referring to.

Thad looked so pleased that he knew something that they

didn't. He lived for moments like that to show that he was intellectually superior somehow. He was going to draw that out as long as he could and let them be confused so he could have a few moments of feeling like he was the smartest person in the room. They all knew that he wasn't —even Thad probably knew deep down—but they let him live out his fantasy for a few moments.

Thaddeus, for all of his faults and failings, was a career performer and enjoyed putting on a show. He paced in front of them dramatically and then started to fill them in on what exactly he was talking about. "Renfield was a character in the original Dracula story and in some of the movies too—most of the movies, actually—in one way or another. In the story, he was a human, but he served Dracula as his master. Renfield was this crazy guy, and I mean *crazy*. He was caged up in an asylum because he was crazy and thought that consuming the blood of living things would give him immortality and all of that."

Once again, the idea of blood being a source of power had come up. That kept constantly happening ever since he looked at some of those books at the start of all of this.

"What does a character in some old novel have to do with anything besides more of your vampire nonsense?" Cedric asked.

"Hey, just stick with me for a minute here. Patience." Thaddeus let them stew for a minute and was obviously enjoying that. "Renfield having a mental disorder that makes him crave the blood of living things was something in the book, but they have actually named an actual mental illness after that character and that kind of condition. In real life. Renfield Syndrome. I read about it online a few times. Some people call it clinical vampirism."

"That's a real thing?" Cedric asked, his jaw hanging open. "It can't be."

"It really is." Thad flashed a broad smile, so happy to have information that none of them had. "Looks like all of those books in the store and all of your Knights Templar connections don't know everything, right guys?"

Jean had to admit that he was a little bit impressed with his apprentice and the kinds of things that he knew. Thaddeus seemed oblivious about so many parts of life, but he absolutely knew all about vampires. There was no denying that.

"So what is that exactly?" Jean asked. "Renfield Disease, I mean."

"It is exactly how it sounds. Just like the character in the book, it is when someone has the desire to feed on blood and sometimes a delusional belief that they are vampires or could one day be vampires if they consume enough blood."

"So, you think this whole group of theirs is suffering from clinical vampirism?" Cedric asked.

"I do," Thad said confidently. "Or something like it, probably. I mean, just look at this!" He pointed out one of the windows on the other side of the room that had been boarded up with planks of wood like all of the others. "They are scared of the sun to the point where they won't even let it into this place. They are living a fantasy, or a delusion or something! It's obvious! We can use that to our advantage."

Jean was more and more impressed by Thaddeus's deductive skills and now was actually surprised that he understood what his trainee meant and saw that it was a great idea. If their enemies believed themselves to be vampires, then they could use that psychosis against them and turn the tables of this whole messed-up situation. They needed to get free, and Jean knew that Thad had figured out a way to try to make an escape.

"Wait until the next time that Mikael comes in," Jean said, nodding to Thaddeus. "And see if he will bring others in with him. If he doesn't, try to give him reason to."

Cedric looked utterly confused and looked at the two of them with wide, blinking eyes. He waited for them to elaborate, but neither of them did, so he was forced to ask himself. "What exactly are you two talking about? Is this some sort of magic secret of yours?"

"No, nothing like that," Jean said honestly. "But magic might come in handy to make it work. It might give us just the edge that we need."

"You are going to use it?" Cedric asked, suddenly looking very worried. "Right here!? Why!?"

"Because it will help us," Jean said. "Don't worry. It's not going to be anything too scary. I think you'll be fine. Actually, I think that you will really appreciate magic a little bit more after we do this since it might just save your life."

Cedric crossed his arms. "Is this how you try to convert people to your vile cause? You make it seem like it is the only way out of a bad situation?"

"It is the only way out of this," Jean corrected. "That is a fact. I'm not asking you to start performing incantations, Cedric. I'm asking you to stay calm while I use just a little bit of power to get us out of this place. Are you really going to make a big deal about that, man? Even if it's the only way? Does all that bullshit the Templar fed you really mean all that much? Is it worth dying for because you won't just accept help from magic? Even indirectly? Grow up. This might be our only shot. You are going to have to put all of your problems aside and let it happen unless you want to die. It's as simple as that."

The young British man did not look very happy to be given an ultimatum like that. He was not at all happy about this plan, even when he didn't even know the specifics yet. Just knowing that magic might be used to carry it out was enough for him to be against it. As much as Jean liked to think that Cedric was on his side in this and that he was not quite like the other Knights Templar, he kept being reminded that those extremist witch hunters had still dug their claws very deep into Cedric's mind and soul. He couldn't help some of his hostility because it had been so ingrained into him that it was almost impossible to shake, even when it might save his life, to accept a little bit of magical assistance. Cedric would not budge, though.

"Fine," Jean said. "You don't have to like it, but if you want to live, just stay out of our way."

Cedric didn't argue with that point. He was not going to

accept help from witchcraft, and he certainly was not going to like it, but he could at least turn a blind eye, if only for a moment or two.

Jean wasn't even sure that Thad's plan would work, but they didn't have a lot of options. Their best bet was to treat their enemies like actual vampires. That was what the Dracule wanted, wasn't it? If they wanted to be vampires so badly, then they could deal with the consequences of being vampires too. They would learn that it was not always a good thing to be living their dreams.

They waited in the room for a few hours until, finally, the door came open, and their captors stepped back inside. Mikael led the way, followed by a few of his other cronies and fellow Dracules. They were all so pale and sickly-looking, like they had not been in the sun in months. They probably hadn't. It might have been years since any of them went out in daylight, depending on how deep their delusional lifestyle went.

Mikael looked them all over with a voracious gaze like they were all just walking pieces of meat instead of living people—if he got his way, they would not be living long anyway. He licked his lips and clicked his tongue, and his smile was broad with excitement.

"So... which one of you would like to be first to have a greater purpose?"

"A greater purpose?" Jean gave a snort of laughter. "And do you mind just elaborating on what the greater purpose would be exactly? I'm curious about the specifics. Is this greater purpose, this higher state of being, all that you are making it out to be? Or—and bear with me on this—is it just some messed up way of you all getting your rocks off to murdering people? That sounds more accurate to me."

Mikael glared at him and stepped right up to him until their noses were practically touching. "It sounds like we may have our first volunteer right here." He then looked past Jean at Cedric. "Or perhaps it is you. The one that brought the sword. That was intriguing. Maybe I should draw your blood with that blade. That might make it even better." He then shifted his attention to Thaddeus, who stayed huddled in the corner, keeping close to the boarded-up windows. "Or maybe it should be you. The fool with nothing to actually offer. The blood pumping through your veins is far more valuable than anything that you could actually offer the world."

Thad initially looked put down but then spoke up just as Mikael was about to make his decision. "It has to be a little embarrassing for you...knowing that vampires are not real but believing that you could be one. You know deep down how crazy that is, right? So, it's embarrassing in one way or another."

"We are preparing for our immortal lives ahead. If one wants to become a vampire, then we must be ready for all that entails. It will take save us time after the transition when our brains will need to be rewired to get used to it. We are preemptively conditioning ourselves for that time. It is the smart thing to do."

"That is smart," Jean said. "But what makes you so confident that you will even be able to find Vlad the Impaler?"

Mikael laughed and pulled out a rolled-up piece of paper from within his jacket. "Because we already have. That's why. The Dracule discovered the location of his remains some time ago, then it was just a matter of finding out how to rejuvenate our lord. Which we also now have. So, with this and the knowledge and blood we have collected, it seems time that we bring him back to this world and he rewards us for our efforts."

"Aren't you nervous that someone already found him? Or that someone will get there first?"

"Most people do not even believe in vampires, so there are not that many people looking. It makes our work much easier."

"But we're looking," Jean said. "Ever since we saw those corpses, we have been trying to figure out what has been going on and why people are dropping dead and having their blood taken. And now we know. So, thanks for that."

Mikael raised a brow and looked very confused. He didn't realize that he was giving them everything that they wanted. Capturing them was a mistake, and he was going to realize that now. He had spent too much time telling them all of the Dracule's dark secrets.

Jean quickly whispered a spell, and the plank of wood on the nearest window was torn off, allowing sunlight into the room. The yellow beam went straight onto Mikael and his allies. The group of them all immediately panicked once the light touched their skin. There did not seem to be any actual physical effects on them; their skin did not burn, and they did not suddenly turn to ash, but that didn't seem to matter. As far as they were concerned, they were vampires being destroyed by their greatest enemy. They scurried to the darker corner of the room, away from the sun's reach. They all looked horrified, and Mikael was suddenly not as confident as he had been before. The sunlight cut right across where they were huddled and where Jean and the others were standing, and it seemed to be a wall that Mikael and the others were not willing to cross. They apparently really did believe that they were vampires. That worked out perfectly for Jean, Thad, and Cedric—who now stared at an open door and an escape route.

They did not waste any time in making a run for it, but Jean made sure to grab the map that Mikael had dropped to the floor in his hurry to find safety in the darkest corner of the room. They would need that where they were going.

The headquarters of the Dracule was in a vacant building, only lit by lamps while all of the natural lighting had been blocked by more and more boarded-up windows. As they ran through the hall, Jean concentrated and performed the same spell again, tearing away the boards blocking the windows and letting the sun in. Screams rang out as the Dracule in those rooms reacted the same way that Mikael had to the sudden light show, and they did not react well. Luckily the chaos and confusion were enough to keep most of them out of the hall and off of the chase, probably cowering in the dark parts of their rooms.

It didn't take too long to find the exit, thankfully. Once they pushed through the door into the outside world, they were safe in the sun's domain, where that crazy cult apparently did not dare to tread. They could hear yells and screams from within that abandoned building, the furious cries of those vampire worshippers as they realized that they had lost their prey.

"So, what now?" Thaddeus asked.

Jean held up the rolled map. "We get to the Impaler before they do and ruin all of their plans. Doesn't that sound good to you guys?"

"It does," Cedric said. "We rid the world of their hopes. If Vlad the Impaler really is a monster, then we cannot let him roam the earth again. The Knights Templar cannot abide that."

"I don't really give a damn what your Templar buddies can abide or not abide by. I just think that people like that should not get the things that they want."

They could all agree on that. It was time to disrupt the Dracule Bloodline's plans.

11

CAVE DIVING

The map was easy enough to follow once they hotwired a vehicle to use to help them travel. Cedric knowing how to steal a car was somewhat surprising, but as always, he gave credit to the Knights Templar for teaching him useful skills.

Before too long, after they had followed the map closely, they all stood at the mouth of the cave opening. After taking so long to find it, they were all just happy to be able to see it, no matter what it was that was actually inside of it. If the Dracule were right, then the remains of Vlad the Impaler were hidden somewhere in the bowels of that dark cavern.

For Jean, he didn't really think that those old bones or ashes were going to spring back to life with some blood, but just in the off chance that all of that was true, it was better to get to the remains of Vlad Tepes before his crazy cult of worshippers did. It was better to be safe than sorry.

Mikael and his followers did not even have a chance to revive an all-powerful vampire conqueror.

They turned on their flashlights and walked toward the maw of the cavern. The darkness waited for them as they approached, but none of them were going to let that imposing unknown deter them away from their goal. They were going to search for Vlad and confirm whether he was there or not.

Just as they came to the entrance of the cave and shined their beams of light inside, there was a sudden sound of screeching. Movement exploded from the darkness as a group of hissing bats flew out from the shadows. Everyone braced themselves as all of the little creatures flapped their wings past them. When the wave of bats moved past them and ascended into the sky, everyone watched them fly away, still a bit startled.

Thaddeus giggled. "Hey, maybe those were vamp—"

"Don't even say it," Jean said. "Maybe they were vampire bats, but I don't think they are going to suddenly transform into a human shape all of a sudden."

"You never know," Thad said. "Either way, seeing a bunch of bats pour out of a cave while we are looking for someone who may or may not have been a vampire seems like some kind of sign, doesn't it? Maybe it is some kind of bad omen or maybe a message from God. You and the Templar are all about God, aren't you, Cedric?"

Cedric didn't answer him, though it wasn't clear if he was ignoring him or just didn't hear him. The Templar knight seemed distracted, his thoughts elsewhere. Jean could tell from his twitching hands that Cedric felt somewhat naked without his shortsword in his grasp. He was still fuming from losing his prized weapon to the Dracules.

They carefully made their way into the cavern. Stalactites hung overhead, and the dark tunnel of rock started off as being quite narrow but then opened up into a larger cave system. It looked much bigger than it had from the view they had outside, but that wasn't too surprising. There was a lot of space beneath the earth that no one would ever be able to see from above.

They were glad to have brought their flashlights since it was the only thing that even made it possible to explore the cave. There was not even the faintest hint of light other than the beams that came from the devices in their hands. With how little light there was, it was probably the perfect place for a vampire to be.

"So, what do we do if we find Vlad?" Thaddeus asked nervously as they walked through the cavern, shining his light around anxiously like he was expecting something to ambush him from the darkness. "I assume that we are not trying to wake him up. So no bleeding on him."

"I doubt we have to worry about him waking up, but no, that's not what we are here for. We get him out of here as quickly as we possibly can. If we take his remains off of the playing field, then maybe the Dracule Bloodline will stop killing people and taking their blood since they won't have a reason to do that anymore."

"I doubt that they will stop there," Cedric said. "People like that—that have devoted their lives to something unnatural like that—will never stop. When something that shouldn't be possible is made possible, the desire to pursue that is too strong. It is just like with magic."

"Can we not argue about magic right now?" Jean asked. "This is a bit more important than your views and your judgment. You know what I think? I think you are just mad that you don't have your sword anymore because now it won't be as easy for you to stab people in the back and to execute innocent people that are just trying to study the most interesting things in the world."

"You can think what you want," Cedric said. "I don't particularly care about your opinion on the matter. I just want my sword back. It had become such a part of me. I don't feel quite right without it. And it definitely does not belong in the hands of people like them."

Cedric's anger was apparent and practically radiated off of him. He took the loss of his sword very personally, like a friend had been abducted or kidnapped.

It was a strange thing to watch since Jean was not sure how to feel about any of it. Part of him was relieved that the weapon was gone since that made it less likely that Mama May's vision of Jean being killed by it would come to pass. It was always nice to feel like you avoided a possible murder. There was still the matter of the ones in red robes that she had seen, presumably the Dracules, so this may have just been the part she had seen about the ones in red robes getting him before Cedric ever had a chance. That could still happen, and maybe all of this was building toward that instead.

"You will be fine without your sword," Jean said. "We're not exactly armed, and we feel just fine. Unless you are planning on engaging in a sword duel with a bat, then you have no real use for it in this cave."

Cedric didn't respond, but Jean could sense that he was still livid as he walked behind him.

"Is it really such a big deal if you lose it? The Knights Templar can't care all that much about one sword going missing. Couldn't they just replace it or something? Let's just move on and be happy that we made it out of that place—sword or not."

Cedric probably wasn't convinced, but Jean didn't care. The missing sword was the least of their concerns at the moment.

They reached a large hole at their feet where the cavern descended further into the earth. The three of them leaned forward and looked down into the abyss. When Jean shined his light to illuminate that pit, it still was impossible to see how deep it went. Cedric took a different approach and picked up a stone off of the ground. He lobbed it into the hole, and they waited to hear it reach the bottom. It took quite a few seconds before they heard the distant ping of that rock connecting with the earth at the bottom of that hole. It was clear that it was a very big drop and would take them a very long time to reach the bottom.

"So, what do you say?" Jean asked, mostly hoping that the

others would be able to convince him to continue onward since he didn't particularly want to have to go down there.

"I say that we don't have the equipment that we would really need to go spelunking down there. We would at least need a rope or something, and we don't even have that. We have absolutely nothing that would make that easier. Without any tools, we would probably just fall to our bloody deaths where no one would find our bodies."

"No one but Vlad the Impaler and the Dracules, you mean. They might find us when they resurrect their vampire overlord with all of that blood that they have been collecting. So at least there is that."

"You're crazy if you think I'm going down there," Thaddeus said. "No, no, no, I can tell you right now that that will not happen. I refuse. If we did that, we would all die. There is no doubt in my mind about that."

They all stood there awkwardly for a long moment in the dark. The flashlights in their hands seemed to be a bit dimmer as their hopes grew less bright.

Thad craned his head to glance at Jean. "Wait a minute, what are we just standing around for!? You have magic! Why not just use it to get us down there?"

Jean laughed until he realized that Thaddeus was being serious about the suggestion and made it sound like it would be so easy. "So, what would you have me do then, Thaddeus? Should I say a few words to conjure up some rope and climbing gear for us? A parachute, maybe for a drop? Would you like me to perform a ritual that would suddenly transport us down there in the blink of an eye?

Or maybe I could say something that would let us gently float down to the bottom at a nice leisurely pace? Which one of those sounds most appealing to you? Just say the word, and the magic will happen at your beck and call."

"Alright, I get it," Thaddeus said. "You made your point. But if you really must know, I would prefer you to give us some big spiral staircase or something that we can just walk down. That would be best."

Cedric seemed disappointed and glanced at them curiously. It really seemed like he expected that something like that would even be possible. It just reminded Jean that Cedric and the other members of the Knights Templar really had no idea how magic worked. They had so little understanding of what real magic even was, but it wasn't like they tried to understand it either and feared it instead. That was why it wasn't at all surprising that Cedric had no idea what Jean's limits were.

"What if you two worked together and did some spell at the same time?" Cedric asked, sounding like an ignorant idiot.

Thaddeus seemed excited about that, but Jean was quick to shut him down. "That's not happening. Not only is something like that not really possible, but if it was, Thaddeus would not be at all ready for it. He hasn't even performed an actual spell yet."

"Only because you've been teaching me with kid gloves so far," Thad whined, sounding like a spoiled and bratty teenager. "It's just book after book so far. When are you going to teach me anything useful? You know, like something that could have helped us get down there."

Jean could have responded with a lot of anger and annoyance, but he took a breath and kept himself composed. He knew Thad well enough at that point to know that trying to argue with him would be pointless.

"Magic not being able to solve every problem is a good lesson for you to learn. As far as us getting down there...the only way to do that will be with our own hands. Will it be dangerous? Of course it will, but this whole thing has been dangerous."

Thad looked back down the pit. "That's more than just dangerous. That's suicide. I thought this whole thing was to investigate a weird murder, and somehow we ended up here, in the bottom of a cave looking for the remains of a man that may or may not be the real-life Dracula! Does anyone else realize how crazy that is!?"

Of course they did, but Thad shouldn't have been all that surprised since the last time that they worked together, they had to fend off ghosts in a haunted house. He should have realized by now that the supernatural elements of the world tended to bring a lot of things that most people would call crazy. That was just part of the job.

Jean stopped waiting for the others to lead the way, and he didn't need permission, so he slowly began climbing into the chasm, clinging to the rocky wall, and was very careful about each move he made on his descent. He could feel Cedric and Thad's gaze on him, probably thinking that he was out of his mind.

Jean looked up at them from where he held himself on the sharp wall of that pit. "Are you two coming or not? Don't tell me you're scared, Cedric. I thought being a real-life knight in shining armor would make you a little more brave."

Cedric looked annoyed by the remark and started to make his way down beside Jean. Thaddeus, unfortunately, was not going to be as easy to pressure into it or convince. He stood perfectly still and refused to follow their lead. He kept staring down into the black abyss and shook his head frantically.

"That is not going to happen. Nope. You guys have fun down there. I hope you don't get mauled by a vampire. Let me know how it goes. I'll be waiting outside where there's not a chance that I will fall to my death."

"Seriously, man?" Jean shouldn't have been surprised, but he didn't think that even Thaddeus could be that much of a coward.

"Seriously!" Thad called back as he walked away, his voice echoing through the cave. A few moments later, he was gone, leaving Jean and Cedric alone, clinging to the rocky walls of the pit.

It was strange to be there in the dark with a man that had once tried to kill him. Now they might both die together, and this cave in Romania could become their tomb.

Thaddeus had no desire to go any deeper into the earth. He

was not in the mood to be stuck down in the dark, especially if it was going to be for the rest of his life. Thad had far too much that he wanted to do in the world to let that be how his life ended. That was not going to happen. He didn't care if Jean approved or not.

As he made his way back through the way they came, he considered whether or not he felt guilty about leaving them behind, but a big part of him did not feel bad about it. It was their choice to jump into that hole. They could have listened to him and avoided it, but they didn't. Of course they didn't because he was never taken seriously. They had all of their old books and secrets, and he was a street magician. That was how they looked at him; it was all they could see. What they didn't seem to realize was that he was smarter than they gave him credit for. They were trapped down there with no way of ever getting out. That was their own fault.

Losing Jean as a teacher would not be good, but he could probably figure out more from all of those books in the shop than Jean had been able to teach him so far. He would find a way to manage and still learn without him if he had to. He still wanted to learn about the real secret powers of the world.

As much as he did not want to, he felt guilt with every step that he took away from them and that he took toward the exit. He tried to push those feelings away, but it was hard not to feel at least a little bit responsible for what happened. He would not have been able to make any difference, though—that was what he had to keep reminding himself.

He kept following the beam of light in front of him, watching his step as he moved through the cavern. He couldn't afford to trip and hurt himself on the way out. He wouldn't have anyone helping him, but at least he was not stuck in a hole. Soon enough, he would be out of that cave and back in the fresh air in places that sunlight could actually reach.

How he was going to get out of Romania on his own was a different kind of discussion, but he would only start worrying about that once he was out of the cave. Maybe he could convince the pilot of that private jet to give him a lift without Cedric being there. He would figure that out once he got that far. For now, escaping the darkness was all he wanted to do.

A sound echoed through the darkness, bouncing off of the cave walls and reached him. He could just faintly make out the sound of voices speaking with one another. It couldn't have been Jean and Cedric, not unless that pit somehow led all the way around to the front of the cavern. That would be one hell of a tunnel—but it probably was not possible. At least, he highly doubted it.

As the voices drew closer, Thad switched off his flashlight and got low, leaning against one of the cave walls to try to stay out of sight. It didn't take long before he could see multiple other beams of light piercing through the shadows around him. The lights moved all around the cave, and whoever was wielding those flashlights was making sure to check each and every inch.

"I do not see them."

"They must be here. They just got a head start, that is all. We will find them. They will pay for what they did."

Thad didn't dare move a muscle, terrified that he might alert them somehow. If he could keep hidden and eavesdrop, then maybe he could figure out something useful to do. He didn't know if he would be able to be of much help to Jean, but the Dracules were heading in that direction. Soon enough, they would reach that big chasm in the floor of the cave and there, they would probably also find Jean and Cedric.

He didn't want to get caught, but he also had to warn them somehow. He had to. He couldn't let them just get ambushed.

Thad got to his feet and tried to hurry back to the pit as quickly as he could without being seen, but he bumped into something in the shadows—something that did not feel like it was a natural part of the cave. Thad stumbled back after colliding with the darkness and looked up at a familiar bald man. It was the member of the Dracules that had abducted him and the others, Piotr, and he flashed that toothy grin that shined even in the dim glow of his flashlight.

"Hello again."

Jean kept trying to focus on what was in front of him—or in this case, beneath him. He and Cedric kept making their slow descent into the blackness below. They had to be very careful with every movement they made, knowing that one misstep could be the difference between life and death. It was going to be a little while before they actually reached any sort of bottom, and it was still difficult to see any sign of one with the shroud of blackness all around them.

With nothing else to do besides slowly descend and with nothing to look at, the best way to pass the time was probably to talk. The problem was that they did not actually have all that much to talk about. Up until a few days ago, they were enemies as far as Jean was concerned outside of that one showing of mercy. Even though they were working together on this search, they were two extremely different people with perspectives that could not be further apart.

"So, do you think we are actually going to find Vlad the Impaler down here?" Jean asked, just deciding to try some small talk that was topical to break the awkward tension that hovered between them. "Or are we going to get ourselves stuck down here for no good reason?"

"Not a clue," Cedric said honestly. "Ideally, it would be brilliant if we could just snatch the remains, put them in our bags, and get the hell out of here. Then I will punch your friend in the face for leaving us here, and then I am going to go my separate way. You go your separate way. And we will all be better off for it in the end."

That sounded fine to Jean—including the part about punching Thaddeus in the face. He deserved it for practically abandoning them there. That was really a cowardly thing to do. He could have at least waited up at the top and checked in on them or given them words of support or something.

There were sounds coming from above them, shifting rock. Jean looked up but still could only see darkness. A strange shape suddenly came down from those shadows above, something thin that almost looked like a snake slithering. The object in the dark shifted past Jean and Cedric. It took a minute for them to both realize that the thing in the dark with them was some long strand of climbing rope. Somehow, Thaddeus Rose had arrived at the right time again and proved why he was always surprising.

"Thad!" Jean called up happily. "Where the hell did you find this!? Is there climbing gear just laying around up there? You perform some summoning spell or something to conjure this rope?"

There was no answer from the darkness above. For a long moment, there was just silence.

Cedric spoke from where he clung to the wall of rocks beside him. "So, either that bastard is brilliant or incredibly lucky. What are the odds of finding exactly what we need? Was this some sort of magic trick?"

"I was joking about that," Jean said. "He didn't use magic, at least not the real stuff. No. Maybe he did one of his old parlor tricks and pulled the rope out of his sleeve or something. I don't know."

They both stared up and waited. Thaddeus must have been having some trouble making his way down. That wasn't too surprising given how scared he was to try going down. It must have taken every ounce of willpower for him to even dare go down, even with the extra support of the mysterious rope.

“Thad!?” Jean called up again.

There was a sound echoing down to them. It sounded almost like a zipper, but Jean realized that it was actually a body sliding down a rope, repelling down toward them. A silhouette came down out of the darkness, and they could make out a blurry figure emerging from the shadows. They slid down the rope but then caught the wall with their feet when they got next to them.

Jean expected to see a smug Thaddeus Rose beside him, but instead, he saw a complete stranger hanging off of the rope. It was hard to make out distinct features in that lighting, but one thing stood out immediately on the man’s face—a V with a vertical line cutting through it.

No wonder Thaddeus was not responding. It had not been Thaddeus at all. It was a Dracule.

“Looks like we caught up to you,” the cult member chuckled. “Good. When we give our lord your blood, it will be very fresh.”

Jean had no intention of giving those psychopaths his blood. He looked back up into the darkness, as if he would somehow be able to see the top now. “Where is Thad?”

“Come with us and find out.”

Jean didn’t budge from the part of the wall where he was holding on for dear life. The Dracule watched him with a great deal of satisfaction.

"Look at you. You can't go anywhere, stuck in the middle of where you started and where you want to go. Cooperate, or I can knock you off of this wall, and you will get down there much more quickly. Would you like that? Come on, let me help you get down then."

The Dracule threw out his foot to kick Jean off of the rocks. Jean just braced himself for the blow but still almost loosened his grip. He couldn't let himself slip and fall. He would die instantly, his body splattered on the cave floor.

"If you do not want me to knock you off, then you have to be cooperative. Do as I say, my friend. You can see your friend." The Dracule looked past Jean at Cedric. "And you can get you your sword back. You will both be very happy. Then we will take your blood, and you will make us all happy. We all win."

"You really think a little bit of blood is going to suddenly bring Vlad the Impaler back to life? You really believe that is going to happen?" Jean knew it was sounding like he was taunting him, but he just was trying to get him to see sense and bring him back to reality; with a member that deep in a cult, though, there was no chance of pulling them out of their fantasy world.

"We will restore our lord to his true power, and in return, he will gift us the immortal life that we all desire. He will give us salvation from death itself, from the weakness of mortality."

His words sounded so drilled into his head. They had probably been drilled into his head along with other Dracule too. Jean wouldn't have been surprised if any of the other members of that cult gave him the exact same answer verbatim. None of them probably really believed it outside of the rewiring that had been done to their thought processes.

More ropes fell down from the darkness above, landing on either side of Jean and Cedric. Soon enough, more of those brainwashed lunatics would descend upon them, and they would be completely outnumbered. There was still a chance to try to get away before they were completely overwhelmed.

"I am going to give you to the count of five, and then I will no longer let you stay there any longer. One... Two..."

Jean didn't let him finish. He knew what he wanted to do. He wanted to get down to the bottom before all of the other Dracules were all over them. That was the goal. Hopefully, Cedric would catch on quickly. More importantly, hopefully, Jean didn't fall to his death to try to carry out his plan.

"Three—"

Jean used any strength he had to fling himself off of the rock wall and grabbed hold of the rope beneath the Dracule. The rope swung wildly to the side, and the cult member let out a terrified yell as they dangled around, bumping into the cave wall. Jean was barely beneath the man, and the Dracule tried to kick him away.

"Are you crazy!? You will get us both killed!"

Jean caught the man's ankle and held on as tightly as he could. The man writhed and swore. There clearly was not going to be enough room on the rope for both of them. Cedric, meanwhile, shuffled as quickly as he could higher up the face of the cave wall and then leaped onto the part of the rope above the Dracule. They had him from above and below, and the man panicked frantically. While Cedric kicked at his face, Jean pulled at his leg. Eventually, it was too much for the Dracule minion to bear, and he lost his grip. He slipped off of the long rope and then plummeted through the darkness, bumping into Jean as he passed by. His cries echoed through the blackness until they heard a crunch when he reached the bottom. He never did finish counting to five.

"Come on," Jean said and cupped his hands together to let himself slide down the rope. He would catch the walls with his feet when things started moving too quickly. Cedric followed him down until they felt solid ground beneath them, having reached the bottom of the abyss.

Jean wasted no time looking at the other long ropes that had been dropped down and that would be used by the Dracules to descend to where they were. They needed to stop that from happening or at least slow them down.

Jean rubbed his hands together quickly and muttered an incantation that he usually only used when he was lighting candles or starting a campfire. All of the ropes suddenly caught fire, and the flames spread quickly up the line. If they were on their way down, they would bump into some serious trouble before they got to the bottom. Their rope would not matter much if there was no rope left.

"Did you just...?"

"Suck it up, man," Jean said. "Eventually, you will thank me and my magic for saving your ass time and time again."

That probably wouldn't happen. Even if he was given great reason to be appreciative, Cedric was incapable of appreciating anything that had to do with witchcraft.

"They probably brought more rope," Cedric said to change the subject. "We should get moving before they regroup. Although there is the matter of how we are going to get out of this place...even if we could climb up, they would just be waiting for us at the top. They probably already killed Thaddeus Rose."

Jean didn't want to believe that, but it was entirely possible. They wanted blood, and that was one way to get it. There was blood now down there too. When Jean and Cedric switched their flashlights back on, they found the body of that Dracule member laying on the cave floor, the spot he had landed after he fell from the rope.

"We can't worry about how we get back yet," Jean said. "We can't. Not before we find what we're looking for. Hell, maybe we can barter our way out with Vlad's remains."

"We can't just hand that over to those crazy bastards," Cedric said. "The whole point of this was to stop them from getting to it first."

"I know, but that might not be so easy anymore. If it comes down to it, we need to be willing to give it up to save our lives."

"Or they will just kill us and take the remains anyway. There is always that option too, eh? How are we supposed to avoid that then? Why don't you just kill them with that disgusting witchcraft of yours?"

"You make it sound so easy, like that would actually be an option. It's not. It wouldn't be that simple, and it wouldn't work. I can't just say a few words and then they all drop dead. You really don't have any idea how any of this works. It's mind-boggling how little you do know about the thing you hate so much."

Cedric crossed his arms and looked up to watch the fire spread up the ropes. He didn't look very impressed with any of it.

"We are wasting time arguing about this. I've given us enough of a head start to go find those remains. We can figure out the rest later."

With that, they hurried past the body of that Dracule and made their way further into the narrow section of the cave. It felt like it was leading to something; hopefully, it would be something worthwhile.

Thaddeus didn't know how Jean had managed to light all of those ropes on fire exactly, but he assumed that was thanks to the magic he knew. Maybe someday he could teach him that spell or incantation or whichever it was. Whatever had caused that sudden scorching was impressive.

Mikael didn't look very happy about it and was not nearly as impressed as Thaddeus was.

"He must have lit it with a lighter or a torch or something!"

"They all were lit at the exact same moment and traveled up the ropes at the same speed! Show me a lighter that can do that, damn you! Get more gear down here! Now! Now!"

The Dracules did as they were told, and they made sure to do it quickly, wasting no time following their leader's orders.

"How is he doing it?" Mikael hissed at Thaddeus. "First those windows were torn open, and now this? He is doing things that should not be possible. How? How is he doing them!? Tell me!"

"What makes you think I know?" Thad asked. He did not owe his captors any answers. "Aren't you all vampires? You guys would probably know better than I do about all of this supernatural stuff."

"You know how he does it, don't you?" Mikael hissed again. "I can see that you do."

"Go down and find out yourself. Maybe he will light you all on fire too."

Mikael suddenly rushed forward and grabbed Thad by the collar. He pulled him close so that Thad caught a big whiff of the man's foul breath.

"I have finally decided which of you I will bleed dry first. It's going to be you."

Thad pushed aside his fear and refused to back down. "All that talk, but I'm still right here. Why don't you tear into my throat then, Big Bad Vampire? Come on then."

"I will," Mikael growled. "Right now, you are a potential bargaining chip. The second that you are not...that is when you will be bled dry. You will become nothing more than a wrinkled husk, and the power inside of you will be given to a far more worthy being."

"You mean good old Vlad, right? Listen, I probably want him to turn out to be a vampire as much as you, but that just seems kind of crazy, doesn't it? The chances of that actually being true? I mean, look at you and your pals. You think that you are vampires, but you are really just a bunch of people suffering from clinical vampirism."

Mikael tightened his grip on him and pulled him even closer. "What are you talking about?"

Thaddeus began going through his whole explanation about Renfield syndrome again. Although as he explained it this time, he found that his listener was not as curious and puzzled as he was angry. The more that Thad talked about the mental condition, the more spiteful Mikael seemed to get. He looked like he was ready to gouge out Thaddeus's eyes if he didn't stop talking. It was all a bit alarming, but he explained it all as best as he could.

"So, you think that we are just madmen? We are aware that we are not yet true vampires, but we will be. Our lord will give us immortality once we bring him out of his desiccation. He will thank us for our loyalty and all of our efforts. Then we will attain all that we want, and no one will be able to stop us."

Mikael pulled Thad toward the dark pit and made him look down into its dark depths. The flames that had burned the ropes were still flickering but starting to fade. Mikael held Thad tightly by the scruff of his neck.

"Your friends have done nothing but prolong the inevitable. They have just delayed us and delayed his awakening. Besides that, they have done nothing but corner themselves like fools. Where do they think that they will be able to go down there? Nowhere. They may find him first, but they won't be able to leave with him. We will rescue our lord soon enough, and then we will feed him."

Thaddeus noticed the other Dracules coming into the cavern carrying strange buckets with harnesses to their backs. All of that blood that they had been collecting from the people they killed was being carted around, being brought for its intended purpose. They really planned to use that blood to revive Vlad the Impaler—and they were going to add Thaddeus's blood into the mix, along with Jean and Cedric's.

Jean and Cedric picked up their pace. It was easy to move quicker knowing that there was someone in pursuit in the darkness behind them. It was very motivating to try to keep away from their enemy for however long that they could.

"Do you really think that they killed Thaddeus?" Cedric asked as they hurried. "I would not be surprised if they did. I doubt that he would put up much of a fight."

"I'm not sure. Thaddeus has a way of winning over an audience."

"So, you think he wowed them with some card tricks, eh? Started pulling rabbits out of hats?"

"I'm saying that nothing would surprise me, and I would not put any of that past him to try."

Jean had a gut feeling that Thaddeus Rose had survived whatever happened above the pit. As easy as it would have been to kill someone like him, he just couldn't imagine the Dracules finishing him off just yet. Thaddeus had a way of coming out on top when he was in dangerous situations. His ambitions were all he cared about in life, and he was going to do anything in his power to make that happen, apparently even avoiding death if it was going to hinder his goals of fame.

Jean and Cedric came to a black wall. They felt around, and there was no way through. They both took a step back, shining their flashlights around.

"This is the end of the line, I guess," Jean said. "It has to be here."

They took a few steps back and started rummaging around the rocks at their feet. Their lights passed over their boots so many times as they grew more and more panicked.

"Maybe we just took a wrong turn, eh?"

"Took a wrong turn where exactly? It was just a straight tunnel. There was no wrong direction to take."

"Perhaps we missed something as we were walking through," Cedric suggested, scratching his chin. "There has to be something that we just didn't see."

Cedric shone his light all around them until suddenly he stopped, his beam of light focused on a spot on the cave wall.

"Wait. What is that?"

He pointed to a hole in one of the walls, barely noticeable in all of the darkness. They both shone their lights on the spot to fully illuminate it, and what they found was certainly interesting.

There was a broken skull, chipped away by time.

"Do you think that this is the Impaler that we are looking for?" Cedric asked.

"No, it's probably the other Impaler, man," Jean said, reaching for the skull. "I would say that this is most likely exactly the Impaler that we are looking for, yes."

Jean gingerly took hold of the skull, a little nervous that the old cranium would crumble to dust in his grasp. Thankfully it seemed like it wouldn't fall apart easily. It actually seemed a little bit strange, actually; something about it felt different than most skulls that Jean had held before—and he had held his fair share of skulls.

The strangest part was not how the skull felt to the touch, though. It was how it looked. There were two long fangs protruding from the teeth on the skull. That was definitely not normal and did give some credence to all of the stories that Vlad the Impaler was actually a vampire.

"Are those fangs?" Cedric asked, sounding tense. "So, all of that was true?"

"It seems so."

"What have you got there?" a voice asked.

They turned and found Mikael and his followers coming down the tunnel. They had obviously found more rope somewhere and had managed to get down that hole.

That was not good.

12

THE SKULL

"That is our lord that you are holding in those shaky little hands of yours."

Mikael and the Dracules did not look pleased that Jean had their idol and hero literally in the palm of his hand. They started to come closer, and with them being at the very end of the cave, there was nowhere for them to run. They were in a potentially literal dead end.

"We would very much like him back. So,\ hand him over."

Jean retracted his arm so it was closer to him and further away from Vlad's followers. He didn't want to just hand it over to that circus of lunatics.

"I think it's probably for the best if I hold on to him for a while," Jean said calmly. "Maybe at least until we are out of this cave. Does that sound good to you guys? Because that sounds great to me."

Mikael was not looking to negotiate. "We will not let you

get in the way any longer. You will hand over that skull this instant, or we will skin your young friend in front of you."

Some of the Dracules pushed Thaddeus forward so that they could get a good look at him. Thad looked understandably concerned, but at least he was still breathing. Jean's instinct that Thad was still alive turned out to be right, but he still was not in a great spot even though he wasn't dead.

As much as he wanted to protect his trainee, Jean knew that it would not be that simple of a choice. "Are we really going to act like this would be a fair trade? You are just going to kill us the second you get the skull anyway. You need to get our blood, right? You'll do to us what you did to all of those other victims of yours. At least be honest about that."

"You are right," Mikael said. "But would you like us to kill him now or spare yourselves a few more minutes of life? The choice is yours, Jean-Luc Gerard. I hope you make the one that you feel is best. Either way, you will still satiate our lord. Now hand him over. Or I kill you, friend." Mikael pulled out the Templar shortsword from within his jacket and grinned at Cedric. "And I will kill him with this."

Jean knew that this was only going to end one way no matter what they did. They were cornered, surrounded, and out of options. The only thing left to do was to surrender, and that was exactly what he did.

Once Mikael and the Dracule had both the skull and their captives, they had what they needed for their revival ritual. Jean was very curious to see the specifics of how they would carry that ritual out. With the amount of blood they had collected from their victim, they must have been preparing for quite a large spell. That much blood would be able to be used to generate all kinds of power, but witchcraft involving that much blood as an ingredient was usually never anything good, and this was no exception. Reviving a centuries-old king was not exactly the most morally accepted kind of spell, especially if Vlad the Impaler really was a vampire.

Those fangs that the skull had seemed to almost confirm that he really was a creature of the night that devoured blood. If that was the case, then maybe their big plan to revitalize him and ask him to make them vampires was not such a crazy and outlandish idea after all.

They would know if Vlad was truly a vampire soon enough, and everyone in the cave seemed to recognize the gravity of that potential discovery. The next few minutes could be what proved the existence of actual vampires, something that could shake the foundation of the world. For the cult of the Dracule Bloodline, this ritual would confirm or disprove all of their firmly held beliefs. The results could potentially upset their group, but even if the ritual did not work, there would still be the true believers that would still think Vlad was a vampire, no matter what the actual evidence said. Some people would always choose fantasy over reality. But if the cult was correct and Vlad Tepes really was a vampire, they would probably feel very validated and think that all of the killings that they committed were justified and worth it. The prospect of that made Jean sick. He hoped that they were wrong so they would not celebrate that.

It wasn't like Jean would have to watch them celebrate, though, since he, Thad, and Cedric were apparently in line to be sacrificed.

Mikael seemed to be able to read his thoughts as his men started preparing the large buckets of blood that they had lugged into the cave.

"We will not be including your blood in the initial restoration ritual. We have more than enough as is."

That might have sounded like it would be a relief, but unfortunately, Mikael was not done speaking quite yet.

"Instead, you three will be our gift to our lord. When he is restored to physical form, he will be famished and looking for sustenance to bring him back to full strength. That will be you. The blood within you will be the nourishment that he needs to fully return to this world."

That somehow sounded worse than being killed like the rest had been. Being served on a platter to a vampire was probably no one's ideal way to go out; it definitely was not Jean's. At least there was a chance that Vlad Tepes was not a vampire at all and that this frisk would not even work. If they didn't end up being Vlad's meal, maybe the Dracules would just let them go. That was probably just wishful thinking, though. More likely, the Dracules would need someone to take out their disappointment on. Jean, Thad, and Cedric would probably be the best way to relieve their frustration.

It was time to see what the future held as the Dracules placed the skull on the cave floor and Dracule members in dark red robes brought in the buckets of blood.

Mikael offered a commentary as he stood beside his prisoners. "The restoration ritual will bring our lord back to the body he had when he was defeated and calcified. It will restore his immortal self to its prime of being thanks to the blood we will anoint his remains with." Mikael turned to Jean specifically. "You are the expert in the occult, are you not? Tell me, what do you make of all of this?"

"I have seen similar blood rituals done but never to this degree. And also, usually, those rituals were done with livestock in sacrifices to bless the land or things like that. Occasionally it was a willing human sacrifice. I can't say that I have seen someone go out and murder people to collect their blood. But I guess that is what a wannabe vampire would do, isn't it? I guess it makes sense."

Mikael smirked at him. "I can tell that you are not fond of our methods."

"You can?" Jean asked wistfully. "What was your first clue? Was it when we tried to investigate the murders you caused, or was it when we tried to stop you from getting the skull? Which one gave it away?"

"You use your sarcasm to try to seem unimpressed. I get it. It must be difficult knowing that you will be given over to him once he returns to this realm."

"*If* he returns, you mean," Jean said. "I don't think it's guaranteed."

Mikael pulled an old, worn scroll out of his satchel and unrolled it. "This right here is our guarantee. The Dracule Bloodline has protected this for hundreds of years. It was crafted by a warlock all those centuries ago, just in case our lord ever fell to the hands of mortals. The instructions, once translated, were quite clear, and we have followed them precisely."

Jean held out his hand. "Interesting. Maybe I could take a look at it?"

Mikael let out a low, cold laugh and pulled the scroll away further out of Jean's reach. "I am sure you would love to get your hands on this. You would probably love to rip it in half, too, but that is not going to happen. You will sit back and watch the splendor of our lord's rebirth. Then, you will help him regain his strength. You can die knowing that you serve a higher purpose to a greater being."

"I would rather just not die at all."

"We all die, so you might as well die for something greater than yourself, no?"

"You say that we all die but isn't the whole point of you reviving Vlad to see if he can turn you into an immortal that is incapable of dying? If you are going to try to make me feel better about being fed to a supernatural creature, do a better job because so far, your sales pitch has not exactly won me over."

"Well, I tried to offer something. Being killed by one of the most legendary figures in history is a great honor. Try to enjoy it as best as you can."

Jean doubted that he would enjoy getting fed upon at all, but time would tell, he supposed. Nothing he said now, no arguments he could make, would be enough to convince this crazy cult to stop this plan of theirs. They were too far gone for any sort of reason.

Now it was just a matter of seeing if there was any truth to this ritual of theirs and any truth to Vlad the Impaler actually being some kind of ancient vampire. Jean would find out soon enough to whatever end. If Vlad really was a monster, then he would devour them. If he was not a monster, then the Dracules would kill them all anyway.

Mama May was right about his future looking rather bleak. The Templar wouldn't kill him; the Dracule would. As far as Cedric being what brought about Jean's doom, in a way, he kind of had. Cedric was the one that got them into all of this mess with the Dracule Bloodline. Jean really wished that he was back home, reading through all of his books instead of living out some horror story; that would have been much more comforting.

"Now. We begin. And our lord is restored to all of his power."

The red-robed Dracules started pouring the blood out of their buckets one by one, spilling it onto the skull on the cave floor. That blood had come from so many different places and so many different people. Jean cringed at the thought of how many people the cult had murdered to get all of that blood. Seeing all of that red, all of those insides being spilled, made his stomach churn.

The skull was dyed red by the blood oozing over it, completely covering it in the innards of all of the people that the Dracule Bloodline had killed. Slowly, the blood pooling around the skull started to bubble and hiss. The liquid twisted and coalesced on the floor and strangely started to solidify, rising up into a more physical shape—the shape of a body.

The old cranium rose as the blood beneath it started to rise up, coming to a standing position with the head on top of the emerging silhouette. The remains started to regenerate as flesh and muscle started to burst out of the bloody shape, coating it and forming a more distinct body than just the silhouette of blood.

The skull's mouth opened, and an unearthly roar came out of it. Skin spread across the bone of the head until it was completely covered, and long strands of black hair grew in seconds on top of it. There was a distinct face appearing now, and the last parts of it that formed were the eyeballs that were filled with hunger and hatred.

Mikael and all of the members of the Dracule bowed before the newly formed man that was trembling and shaking in front of them. He looked at his hands and down at the rest of his body. He seemed so amazed by his own body that so far, he had not seemed to notice that there were even any other people around him. Slowly, he straightened his posture, and the infamous Vlad Tepes stood proudly in front of them all.

"My lord," Mikael said from where he was bowed. "The Dracule Bloodline has waited a very long time for this day. Everything that we have tried to accomplish, that everyone has worked so hard for, has been to make this moment possible. We have awaited your awakening, done everything in our power to make it possible. And here we are. Here you are."

The mere presence of Vlad the Impaler was different than anyone else that Jean had ever been around. He didn't seem like another person. Just looking at him felt more like he was looking at a rumbling storm or a tornado or some other force of nature; it was hard to describe, but he just seemed like so much more than his physical appearance. There was real power within him that his flesh could barely contain.

Vlad still did not seem to really pay anyone else any mind, even Mikael, as he was proclaiming his undying fealty to the beast that had just been revived. His eyes were wide and were constantly rolling in their sockets since he couldn't seem to focus his attention on any one thing in particular. He looked crazed, and most especially, he looked starved. All of that blood they had given him to revive him and get him moving again did not seem to be enough. He wanted more, and he probably would not stop until he had his fill.

"We are ready and waiting to serve you, my lord," Mikael said proudly. "You need only say the word, and we shall obey you, assist you however we can."

A demented grin stretched across Vlad the Impaler's face, showing off his long fangs. Suddenly, moving quicker than anyone in the cave could really comprehend, he snatched a nearby Dracule and bit into his neck. The cultist let out a shriek as the vampire fed on him wildly, tearing open his throat when he pulled away to move on to his next meal. The agility with which he moved was absolutely inhuman and should not have been possible, but his undead body did not seem to care about what was possible and what was not. The ritual that restored him to flesh should not have been possible either, but there he was, tearing apart all of his followers one by one.

Jean grabbed hold of Thad and Cedric's backs, gently pulling them back away from the sudden carnage that was breaking out. He tried to get as much distance as possible between them and the monster that was cutting through people like butter.

If they could get away from him and make it out of the cave alive, it would be a miracle. The only real chance was if he was distracted by other people. The Dracules were panicking, trying to scatter in the cramped cave, but it was not doing them any good. The Impaler pounced on them before they could get very far. Soon enough, he would have torn through all of his followers and would move on to Jean and the others next.

"We just need to get outside," Jean whispered, but they couldn't hear him since gunshots rang through the cave.

Some of the Dracules had apparently woken up from their delusions enough to try to stop their bloodthirsty feral idol. A few of them had pulled guns out and fired any bullets they had into Vlad, but the beast barely even seemed to notice the projectiles putting holes in him, and they didn't seem to slow him down at all either. He continued to tear apart all of his worshippers.

Still, there were some that remained devoted even as they watched the carnage taking place around them and should have seen how useless it was to try to speak with that fiend. He did not care about negotiation or about reasoning; he apparently only cared about consuming as much blood as possible, and he didn't care whose it was.

Mikael apparently had not quite accepted that fact and stepped toward his monstrous idol, his arms outstretched pleadingly and Cedric's sword still in his hand.

"My lord! My lord! We have brought others to satiate you! Ones that have not served you faithfully! Please stop! We have never abandoned you! Or forgotten you! Do not punish those who have never failed you! Reward us! Make us like you!"

Mikael was apparently oblivious to the fact that Vlad the Impaler was clearly not going to give him what he wanted. He had no intention of ever giving them immortality or sharing his power with them. He was showing his gratefulness to them by devouring them and wouldn't stop until he was appeased, until that hunger abated. It didn't matter what Mikael or any of the others said because when it came down to it, they were just walking slabs of meat for him to consume.

Mikael continued to approach the monster as he tore into one of his fellow cultists. He got much closer to that abomination than most people probably would ever dare to or probably ever should.

"My lord! Enough! Please! There is no need for any of this! There is no need to—"

Like an animal being interrupted during its meal, Vlad suddenly turned toward Mikael and snapped at him with incredible speed. He bit into Mikael's arm and then tossed him aside. The leader of the Dracules was hurled through the air and hit the cave wall hard. The Templar sword slipped out of his hand and clattered to the rocky floor beside him.

Just as they were about to slip away, Cedric saw what happened and moved toward Mikael and his sword. Jean managed to get a hold of his arm before he could.

"What are you doing!?"

"I'm getting my sword back!" Cedric snapped while trying to pull his arm out of Jean's grip. He had made it clear how bothered he was by his sword being taken but retrieving it meant getting very close to that ravenous fiend.

"You'll be killed!" Jean hollered over the chaos around them. "It's not worth it!"

"You have no idea what that sword is worth! Especially to me!" Cedric threw a punch that connected with Jean's gut, knocking the wind out of him.

Jean fell back a bit, letting go of Cedric. The Templar knight immediately ran from him toward the direction of Mikael and the sword. Jean wheezed and held his stomach, trying to breathe right again, but it wasn't exactly easy. He didn't know why he even bothered trying to stop Cedric from going to get his sword. That young man wasn't going to be persuaded by anything anyway. Besides, it was not like they were friends. Cedric was more of a reluctant ally for the time being but would probably go back to trying to destroy witchcraft when all of this was done. That sword that he wanted would probably be used to kill practitioners of magic in the future, so maybe it wouldn't be so bad if Cedric got torn apart by the vampire like the rest of the bad guys were being.

Cedric did not care if he was risking his life to get his sword back. Just being in that cave was life-threatening as it was, so it wasn't all that different.

That sword meant more to him than anyone could possibly understand. It was the physical evidence of all of the time and energy he spent to become a full-fledged member of the Knights Templar, a testament to his accomplishments. Most importantly, it was his personal weapon against the evils of the world, one that he proudly wielded to serve the Templar. He had been foolish to let those cultists even get their grimy hands on it, and now that he had a chance to get the blade back, he was going to take it.

Jean could try to stop him all he wanted, but Cedric had no obligation to listen to him. If he had done his job properly back at the Winchester Mystery House, Jean would not have even been there to try to stop him, and who was he to even try? He always talked about how the Knights Templar knew nothing about witchcraft, but people like him knew nothing about the Templar either. If he did, he would have known why that sword was so important and was not something that Cedric was just willing to leave behind.

Cedric watched his step as he jumped over fresh bloody corpses and sharp rocks to get to the other side of the chamber. He tried not to focus on the murders happening a short distance away, and when he glanced to make sure

Vlad's attention was not him, he really regretted looking over at all. The vampire's jaw was clamped onto one of his cultist's necks, and he was ripping into it like a wild animal to the point that the Dracule's head was torn off and fell to the cave floor. That sight made Cedric move even more quickly, and he just prayed that he would not be the next one that Vlad set his sights on. Cedric would prefer to keep his head firmly on his shoulders.

When he reached Mikael lying in a heap, he could see his Templar sword resting beside the unconscious cultist. Cedric went to reach for it when Mikael suddenly threw his hand out and caught his wrist before he touched the hilt. Mikael looked up from where he lay, smiling up at him.

"You are not going to get out of here alive. None of you are. My master will feast upon you."

"Aye, maybe, but I think he's a little busy feasting on all of you first."

Mikael sneered and squeezed harder. He suddenly climbed to his feet and grabbed hold of Cedric. He was a big man and physically stronger than Cedric, even with one of his arms bleeding from where his vampire overlord had bitten him. He put Cedric in a stranglehold and started pulling him toward Vlad, who was busy ripping apart another Dracule member.

Cedric had just managed to get ahold of the sword as he was pulled away, but the hold that Mikael was restraining him with made it practically impossible to be able to swing the sword effectively; his arms were pinned to his sides, and the tip of the sword was pointed at the ground where it would not do him much good.

Mikael heaved him over to the vampiric beast in the cave. "My lord! You see!? Look what I have brought you! This man is a member of the Knights Templar! A holier sacrifice than your own legion, to be sure!"

Vlad dropped the body that he was eating and turned to Cedric and Mikael with some curiosity. He had been such a feral monster since awakening, so they hadn't had much of a chance to see him standing still. So far, he had been a blurred flash of death as it came for the Dracule Bloodline one by one. Now though, he stood more still than he had, and Cedric got a better look at the ancient figure's face.

Vlad's mouth was open, showing those fangs, but the entire lower part of his face was messily stained with blood, coated by the insides of a number of different people that he had murdered in just the few minutes since his unholy resurrection. He looked tantalized, excited by the possibility of feasting on more people. It was horrifying to behold, a true abomination.

The Knights Templar was sworn to destroy such unnatural and vile things, but up until that point, he had only ever encountered people that were dabbling in sacrilegious witchcraft. Those people were sinful and disgusting, but this creature in front of him was on a whole other level. None of the Templar teachings or trainings could have prepared him for an encounter with something like that. While the Knights were well aware of supernatural forces at work in the world, vampires were talked about as a serious possibility. There was no denying that this demon was a vampire either. There was no argument to be made that it was just a case of clinical vampirism or Renfield syndrome or any of that because none of those explanations accounted for this creature's abilities. His fangs had not been fake. His speed was unbelievable and humanly impossible. He could shake off bullet wounds like they were nothing more than mosquito bites.

This being in front of him was a product of unholy powers, probably some form of witchcraft similar to whatever words were spoken to restore his body minutes ago. The monster was just another example of the dangers of magic and why it should be purged. Beings like that, undead monstrosities, should not exist in any capacity. Their presence in the world was a stain on God's handiwork, and it was exactly the kind of thing that proved why the Knights Templar was needed. If anything, it reaffirmed Cedric's commitment to their crusade and to the paths that he swore. There was so much evil in the shadows of the world, and they needed to be rooted out and destroyed—starting with the foul thing that looked at him hungrily.

Mikael pushed Cedric closer to the beast, and Cedric did everything he could to try to break out of the bond that he was in. If he could just get one of his arms free, especially the one with the sword, he could get Mikael off of him without much issue. But he was just completely overpowered.

Cedric glanced over and saw that Jean and Thaddeus were still waiting by the entrance to this part of the cave. He wished they would do something, but he also was not going to beg for their help. He didn't want to give Jean the satisfaction of being right about the risks of trying to get the sword. The last thing he wanted to do was give a practitioner of witchcraft a reason to say "I told you so" to him. He shouldn't ask sinners that knowingly consorted with dark magic for help. They were not his friends, and they were not really his allies. They were not much different than the abomination that he was being pushed toward.

Vlad took a step toward him, licking his bloody lips.

"Yes!" Mikael laughed, his voice ringing bedside Cedric's ear. "Yes! This is the kind of meal you really want! I am sure it will taste much better than our blood!"

Vlad came very close, and his face twisted with anticipation, ready to bite down on Cedric at any second—but he didn't get the chance.

Jean yelled out something, words that Cedric didn't recognize that bounced off of the walls and filled the chamber with an enormous echo. The ceiling of rock above them cracked and split open, pouring enormous slabs of earth down directly over Vlad's head. The vampire hissed and snarled, trying in vain to get out of the way as he was buried beneath the rocks.

Mikael had loosened his grip when he was startled, and that gave Cedric just enough time to break free of his grasp. The second his arms were free, he lunged with his sword. It felt good to have his blade back in his hand as he drove it into Mikael's gut. The Dracule leader let out a gasp as the metal pushed through his stomach, choking out blood and looking at Cedric with shock before falling on his back, the sword sliding out of him as he collapsed. He gargled on his own blood as it bubbled in his mouth. It was a bad wound, one that he would not survive.

Cedric made sure that he had a chance to say what he wanted to say to him before he bled out. "This sword belongs to me, eh? You never should have taken it. You see where your vile machinations got you? You killed all of those people to summon a devil to this earth. You will burn in the pits of Hell for this. And when you do, remember my face as the one that sent you there. Or who knows, maybe your vampire ruler will make you like him before you die. I doubt it. He looks preoccupied. By the power of the Knights Templar, your evil has been banished from his world." Cedric genuflected with his sword and then started to walk away from the dying man and the buried impaler.

The mound of stone that Vlad had been buried under started to shift, and Cedric looked back at it with horror. No one should have been able to get out from under there, at least not without some sort of excavation equipment, but once again, Vlad the Impaler was showing that he was not human. With that kind of strength and fortitude, he was something else entirely. A real vampire.

Jean and Thad called over to him frantically, waving their arms around. "What are you waiting for!? You got the sword, so hurry the hell up and get out of there! Come on!"

Cedric jogged over to them, past the bodies of the Dracule Bloodline. Most of the cultists had been killed in the slaughter, probably wishing that they had chosen another line of work. They probably would have preferred one where the man they deified did not start feeding on their flesh and draining them of every drop of blood in their bodies. Cedric thought it was fitting; there was justice to them being punished by their own evil. They should never have tried to utilize such power, but their desire for immortality blinded them to the horror they were unleashing upon themselves.

Cedric would not thank Jean for collapsing the ceiling down on Vlad with magic. He was not going to show gratitude when he had used witchcraft to make it happen.

"Great, you got your sword back," Jean said. "So let's get as far away from here as possible."

That sounded fine to Cedric. Hopefully, that vile thing would stay buried long enough for him to bring back more knights to come to help him completely erase it from the world.

It seemed he wouldn't have to wait that long as the vampire managed to lift the rocks off of himself, heaving them out of his way like they were made of paper and setting himself free from the collapsed ceiling. He tossed one of the slabs of stone right into the wounded Mikael, who was crushed instantly under the weight of that enormous piece of stone.

"Go, go, go," Jean whispered frantically, trying not to draw the creature's attention.

Cedric was not going to argue with him about that, not when it was a matter of survival. They hurried toward the direction of the exit of the cavern, back in the darkness. The screeching of that inhuman monstrosity behind them echoed through the cave.

13

THE HOPE FOR THE DAWN

Jean didn't care about trying to recover Vlad the Impaler's remains anymore. The people that he wanted to stop from getting it were all either dead or in the middle of dying, so he no longer had to worry about the Dracule Bloodline getting their hands on it. The most obvious difference now was that those human remains were running around trying to eat him and his colleagues.

The three of them sprinted through the darkness of the cavern, trying to get back to the outside world as quickly as possible. Escape did not seem likely, though, not with an actual real vampire probably hot on their trail hunting them down. They probably would not be able to outrun something like that, so they needed to be prepared for the worst.

"You're the vampire expert," Jean said to Thad, panting as he ran. "Don't you have any bright ideas how to get rid of that thing?"

"I only know what the movies have told me, and the weaknesses always differ! It could be any number of things, or it could be nothing at all, and all of those films could have been wrong!"

Jean knew it was a long shot, but it was really all they had. He doubted that the magic he knew would be able to do much good against him, and he also didn't think that Cedric's sword would make much of a difference in a fight. They needed some kind of advantage, some weakness that they could exploit. He knew some of the basics offhand but not nearly as well as Thaddeus.

"Let's just say one of them is right. What kind of things are we looking at potentially, Thad? Sunlight obviously, but what else?"

Thad tried to answer through heavy breathing, exhausted from the running. "Yes, sunlight is usually the most consistent weakness. You could also drive a wooden stake through his heart, maybe. Or remove his head and burn the body. Or stake him into his coffin. Or rip out his heart. Or feed him garlic? Or fend him off with a holy item like a crucifix or something."

That was a lot of "or's" without any real concrete answer of the best way to get rid of him, but that was just like Thad had said. There were tons of ways to supposedly do it, but very few were exactly alike. There was no easy and foolproof way to get it done.

"No one has any garlic or wooden stakes lying around, do they?" Jean asked. "Because that would be the best timing ever if you did."

"Sadly, no," Thad said. "I must have left all of my vampire-slaying gear in my other purse."

All they had was Cedric's sword from the Knights Templar that he loved so much, and there was no guarantee that a normal blade like that would even be able to do anything to that monster. Given how little bullets and giant rocks actually did to Vlad, it was unlikely that a normal blade would be able to do any real damage.

If their luck held, then he might be too busy finishing off his legion of doomed followers to pursue them. Unfortunately, they had not been that lucky at all on this venture.

The hisses and roars from that creature echoed behind them, and they sounded much closer than before. Evidently, Vlad the Impaler has no intention of letting any of his prey get away. He was going to hunt them down before they had the chance to leave that terrible cave. He must have been moving quickly because they could hear movement coming from the darkness at their backs. With the speed that he had shown when he massacred the Dracules, he would be caught up to them in no time at all.

Jean thought he could see the cave open up far ahead, but it was difficult to tell since it was dark outside too. Without the sun shining—if it was even a weakness—he could chase them outside of the confines of the caverns too. Things really were not looking good for them, and they were about to look worse.

The sound of a stalactite falling alarmed them all and prompted them to look over their shoulders. At first glance, it didn't seem like anyone was behind them, but then they saw a shape moving above, right along the ceiling of the cave. It was Vlad, sprinting along the roof of the cavern, upside down, but that did not seem to make a difference at all to him. He cackled maniacally, apparently enjoying the thrill of the hunt as he drew closer to his prey.

"Keep moving!" Jean yelled. "I think the exit is just ahead!" He was not even sure if that would make a difference, but just the hope that it might could help push them forward more quickly. They would see what happened when they actually got out. For now, they just needed to focus on leaving the growing shadows of that cave and the death that it had spawned.

They were so close to the mouth of the cave. The vampire running above them was a bit distracting, though, and a bit alarming too. If one of them tripped over the jagged terrain and fell behind, they would probably be eaten next. They had to be so very careful, or that was the end for them.

They could hear Vlad the Impaler's excited snarls as he ran above them. It sounded like he was directly over their heads, but nobody wanted to look up, not when they were so close to being out of that cavern finally.

Just as they reached the opening of the cave and could see the outside world, Vlad suddenly landed right in front of them. That brought their escape to a grinding halt as he loomed in front of them and blocked their exit route. His long black hair dangled in front of his face, partially obscuring his features, but they could still see all of the blood around his mouth and the hunger in his eyes.

"Guys..." Thaddeus's voice trembled, probably realizing that it could very easily be the last days of his life. "This...this is legitimately Dracula. The *real* Dracula. We...we are about to get killed by Dracula...how many people can say that, right? That's pretty special, at least. Yeah...Dracula. Wow." Thad slowly raised his hand to give an awkward wave. "It's an honor and all that, Dracula, sir."

Vlad the Impaler glowered at them, and his piercing gaze swept across them like he was trying to decide which to focus on and which one he wanted to start with. He could attack them at any second, and with his speed, they might even die before ever realizing what had happened.

Then a flicker of hope arrived—a prick of light shone over Vlad's shoulder, peaking over a mountaintop. Night was apparently nearly over. They had spent the whole night in that cavern, and now dawn was approaching. If they could buy time until the sun rose, then maybe they might have a chance of surviving this whole ordeal.

The sun. Of all of the weaknesses of vampires depicted in fiction, that was the most common way to kill those monsters, according to Thaddeus. Hopefully, that would prove true in real life, too, because it was the only weapon that they had. It had to work, or they were all dead.

Cedric nudged him gently, signaling that he also saw it. If they were going to make it out of this encounter alive, they would have to put all of their differences aside and use everything at their disposal.

"You are not what I expected," Jean said, trying to buy time. Hopefully, Vlad enjoyed listening to conversation, even if he didn't seem to enjoy engaging in it. "I did a lot of research on you recently. And there were a lot of different opinions about you all over the place. None of them described you like this, though. I expected a bit more elegance."

Vlad stared at him, still breathing heavily, looking ready to strike. He didn't speak for a second; it looked like he wanted to.

"So have you always been this way, or is this a byproduct of some botched resurrection? I would hope it's the latter, but who knows, maybe you were just born this way."

The sun was rising but not nearly quick enough. They needed it up immediately, high enough where the light could reach, where it hopefully could shine on Vlad and save them all, but it might be too slow to work.

Vlad hissed and opened his mouth wide, showing his fangs. He was ready to strike.

Cedric knew they needed time, but they also needed to survive. That meant defending themselves as best as they could, even if they knew that they did not stand a chance. They had to keep surviving and not let Vlad kill them yet. They just needed to last a little bit longer.

Just as it seemed that Vlad was going to rush them, Cedric drove his sword into Vlad's chest. If they were luckier, that would have been enough, but of course, it wasn't. The metal went straight through him, and he didn't look bothered by it at all. The vampire didn't even wince. He just looked down at the sword in his torso and let out a gross cackle. He seemed to be enjoying the attempt on his life, probably very pleased that it had no effect on him whatsoever. His immortal life would not be taken by that kind of weapon. The sun probably really was the only way to get rid of him—he really hoped so, at least, because something needed to work.

Vlad, with the sword still lodged in him, reached out and took hold of Cedric's throat. He could probably snap his neck with ease or tear it clean off, but before he could, Jean started chanting one of the only spells he knew how to use in combat—one for levitation. He focused his attention on Vlad, and the vampire suddenly floated off of his feet. He hovered a few feet off of the ground.

Vlad the Impaler had probably been through a lot in his life, more than most people realized, probably thanks to being a vampire. But Jean doubted that he had ever been lifted into the air against his will by a magic spell. Jean was happy to introduce him to a new experience and provide him with something he had never been through before, especially when that meant protecting them and buying more time for daybreak to come.

Vlad looked confused, hissing and seething, as his body was suspended by nothing. He probably could not even fathom what was happening to him in that moment. He was probably more shocked that he was not able to feast upon them without resistance like he did with most people. He could not have been used to having actual obstacles stand in the way of him and his food.

Vlad Tepes roared with furious determination, desperate to break free of magic holding him back. He just floated there, bearing his fangs and looking like he wanted to shred them all to pieces. If he managed to get down from there, he would make them pay for daring to stand in his way.

Who were they to stand against one of the most dangerous figures in the history of mankind? Who were they to stand against an immortal beast that slaughtered their kind in droves? Vlad had butchered men like them, and he had impaled them and skewered them across fields, and he probably wanted to do the same to them. He would. Jean could feel him trying to break free. That vampire's strength was even breaking through the magic. Jean couldn't hold him up there much longer.

Light met Vlad up there, and the sun touched his face. The vampire's head started steaming and peeling away as he hissed in pain. He writhed and shook from where he was suspended in the air. Dawn had come, and the sun was burning Vlad the Impaler away, piece by piece.

It turned out sunlight being fatal to vampires really was something that carried over into reality. That yellow star had no remorse and showed that vampire no mercy. Vlad Tepes had only just returned to the world after centuries of being in the dark. But now that he had seen the light, he was leaving again. That great warrior had come back for one last battle, but now his time had come. Vampire or not, death had come for him.

Vlad's body burned, and he fell out of the air as Jean released the levitation spell. The Impaler lay in a burning heap as his newly reformed body was burned away to nothing right before their eyes.

None of them had ever been so happy to see the morning sun before. If that had not worked, they would all probably be getting fed upon at that very moment. Instead, they were alive and well and watching their enemy turn to dust. They had won. The murderous cult was gone, and their monstrous vampiric idol had been destroyed. The day was already off to a good start.

Mikael did not want to die. He especially did not want to die at the hands of someone that he believed was going to give him immortality. Instead, Vlad Tepes had given him the opposite of what he had hoped for. That monster was the one that had brought death when he should have been the one that gave them all even more life.

The Dracule must have meant nothing to him. Their loyalty and devotion to him as their master was ignored, even after offering him others to satiate his inhuman hunger. That should have been enough. There should have been no reason to slaughter his dutiful subjects.

Now Mikael could feel the blood leaving his body. He regretted many of the choices that he had made in his life, especially the ones that brought him to that moment. He could see his greatest mistakes flash through his mind and remembered how all of those many decisions were all made to reach a certain goal. He had gotten there and crossed the finish line, but his result was not what he was hoping it would be. There was no reward at the end of the long road like he thought there would be. Worst of all, there was no immortality.

Mikael had dedicated his years, so many years, to finding Vlad and reviving him. He had helped get all of the necessary materials for bringing Vlad back into the world. He had made all of that even possible, and the only thanks that he got for it was being killed like his loyalty and dedication meant absolutely nothing. All of that time had just been a waste. He had burned through so many years trying to create more years for himself, but all he had actually managed to accomplish was destroying the years he already had. He had thrown his life away in foolish pursuit of more life. He could not believe his own idiocy, but now he was paying for it.

The thing that they had brought into the world was a real monster, just like all of the stories said. There was evidently a difference between worshipping the idea of a vampire versus actually being able to serve the vampire itself. An idea could not tear you to pieces in seconds, but a physical being could. The Dracule had brought it on himself. Vlad Tepes was not appreciative of their hard work. He just seemed to appreciate the blood in their bodies. That blood seeped out of Mikael's body and spread out over the dark rocks of the cavern.

After all of the blood that Mikael had helped to collect in the name of his vampiric lord, it was only fitting that his own blood was being stolen from him. He could practically hear the laughs of his victims echoing throughout the darkness of the cave around him. This was karma and justice for all of the awful things that he had done.

Mikael wanted immortality, but he would never get it now. No, his mortality was feeling more real than ever. Death was coming for him—more than that, it had actually found him. He could see its dark shadow encroaching him and could feel an unearthly cold air wrapping around his body. The warmth of life, the bright vibrance of the prospect of immortality, could not protect him now. There was no prolonging his life now, and there was no escaping death. He was just like most other people.

His greatest fear had come, and he could only lay there and face it. His time in the mortal world had come to an end, and he regretted what his life had become.

As Mikael's life ended, blood continued to spill out of his body and joined the rest of the blood of the members of the Dracule Bloodline that filled the cave.

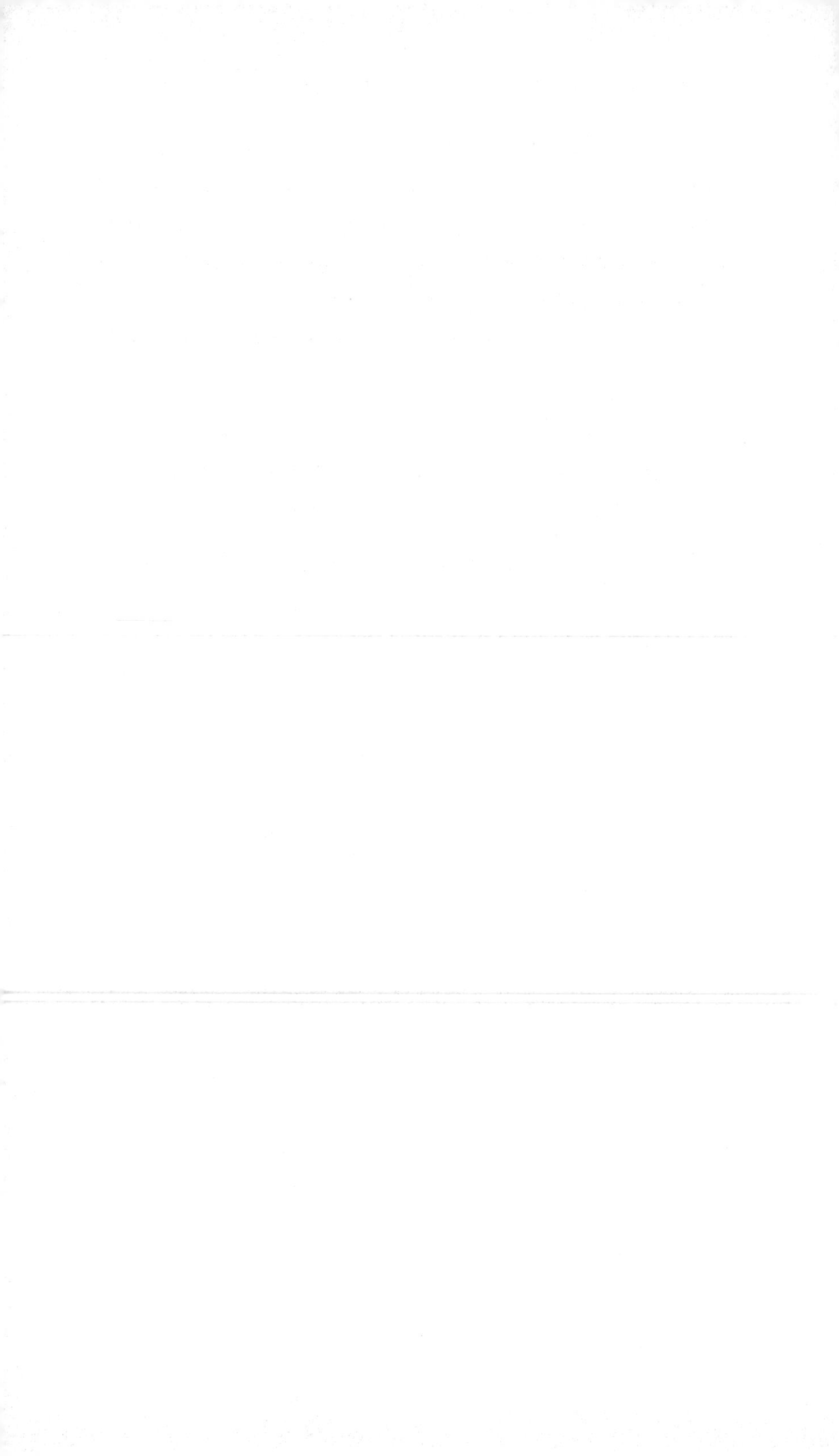

14

THE BATS THAT FLEW AWAY FROM TRANSYLVANIA

As they basked in the sun, Jean dug through the newly made ash pile outside of the cave. He plucked out that strange skull and examined it. Those fangs still protruded from its teeth, but they now looked much less threatening when they weren't covered in blood and attached to a shrieking immortal madman. He was just glad that the vampire was dead. He would make sure to keep blood far away from that skull, just in case it started to try to form itself a body again.

There was one other thing in the ashes—the sword of the Templar that Cedric cared about so much. He pulled that out by the hilt and offered it back to its owner.

"I believe this is yours."

Cedric looked a bit surprised but took it. "Thank you. I appreciate it."

"That was way too close, guys..." Thad said, his hands on his head. "But we did it. We really beat Dracula. The actual, honest to God, legitimate Dracula. What do you think sounds more impressive? We defeated Vlad the Impaler, or that we defeated Dracula? They both sound cool, right? I am definitely going to tell my audience about this. They will love it. Ghosthunter. Vampire slayer. You guys are really helping me build up quite the skill set. I appreciate that."

They weren't doing it solely to help make Thad's ego grow bigger and bigger, but that was an unfortunate side effect of their success and how well they worked together. Thaddeus was not wrong about that part of it. They had exorcised the ghosts in the Winchester Mystery House, and now they had destroyed a centuries-old legendary vampire. They had to take a little pride in victories like that. They had accomplished things that most people wouldn't ever think would even be possible.

"So..." Jean turned to Cedric. "We solved your mystery, and we put a stop to it. And that doesn't even cover all of the other horrific things that happened during that time too. So, I suppose we are even now then."

"I suppose we are," Cedric said, but something seemed off about him.

"Is something wrong?"

"It is just that I am tired of seeing all of these unnatural occurrences take place."

"I figured you would be happy," Jean said and tapped the pile of ash with his foot. "Since you managed to help get rid of something like this. That will probably make your bosses in the Knights Templar very happy, won't it?"

Cedric didn't seem too sure about that. His superiors must have been difficult people to please.

"Thank you for your help, Jean," Cedric said glumly. "I appreciate your assistance."

"I hope it will be the last time. You can understand why spending time with you is not very relaxing. So, at least give me a few years before I have to see you again. Maybe by then, I will have forgiven you for trying to cut my head off."

"Once we get back, I don't intend to see you again," Cedric said.

That sounded perfect.

The three of them mostly just slept on the flight back away from Romania. The sunlight poured through the windows, and Jean loved feeling its warmth against his skin. It was so invigorating and comforting, like an unseen blanket wrapping his body. It probably felt much better to him than it had to Vlad the Impaler when he felt the sun touch his skin.

They all silently celebrated the fact that it was over and that they had all survived. Things had seemed pretty uncertain when they were being chased through that cave, but somehow they had managed to make it out in one piece. The same could not be said for the Dracule Bloodline, but none of them felt very bad about that. That was the cult's own fault.

Once they landed, it felt good to be home, and Cedric quickly departed, wasting no time in leaving. He didn't want to spend any more time with them, probably afraid that their enjoyment of witchcraft was contagious and that he would somehow be corrupted. It was just as well. Jean and Thad immediately felt better once that man and his sharp sword were out of sight. Hopefully they would never have to deal with him or the Knights Templar ever again.

15

THE WAITING REDEMPTION

Cedric knew that he should feel proud of what they had been able to do. It was the goal of the Knights Templar to eliminate evil and unnatural threats from the world, and that was exactly what he had done. He had helped to vanquish that ancient monstrosity before it had a chance to unleash itself upon the unsuspecting world. What greater example was there of stopping evil than slaying a vile creature like that? Most of the other knights in the Templar probably had not done something like that and instead had only probably ever tracked down people practicing witchcraft. Those people, despite their failings and their sins, were still human beings. They had just been corrupted and misguided by power that they should never have. This beast, a real vampire, was not human and could have potentially been a plague upon the earth.

Vlad the Impaler had been warped into that by some sort of dark magic, and his followers used magic to restore him.

More and more, Cedric was starting to see the scope of the potential danger that magic posed, and it was much larger than he could ever have imagined. It was not just people performing little spells to improve their place in life or to mess up the lives of one of their neighbors. They weren't just using magic to make someone fall in love with them or something juvenile like that. Some of them no doubt were, but there were others that had attained truly terrifying power. Some could bring back abominations from the dead using the blood of innocents to do it, and there were probably many others in the world that had done something similar, and it was not just limited to the Dracule Bloodline's unholy cult. It couldn't have been.

Any practitioner of witchcraft could probably attain those same secrets and that same power. That was exactly why the Knights Templar was so dedicated to purging the people that would wield that kind of power. But after what Cedric saw in Romania, dark magic had gone unchecked more than even the Templar probably realized. They didn't know that magic could use sacrificial blood to create or revive creatures like Vlad the Impaler. Vampires had slipped completely beneath their notice, but for all they knew, there could be more out there and it was not just limited to Vlad Tepes and the truth of his connection to Dracula. There could be others like him, just lying dormant in the darkness, waiting for blood to allow them to rise again. This might have only been the start—and that was horrifying to think about.

If Vlad had not been stopped there, at that cave, if the sun had not risen when it did, the whole planet could have been in jeopardy against something like him. Bullets and blades could not stop him. He had even been crushed under rocks that would flatten most men, and it had done nothing; it had barely even slowed him down. The sun was the only thing that finally took him down and burnt away his newly restored invulnerable body, leaving only the charred skull behind. Cedric still wasn't sure how he really felt about Jean taking the skull. As far as they knew, it could still be used to restore him again if another blood ritual was enacted. It seemed risky to not just destroy the skull and be done with it.

There was the matter of Jean-Luc Gerard in general. That man had an encyclopedic understanding of the occult and the supernatural and was a practicing warlock. By all intents and purposes, by the judgment of the Templar, he should be executed for his heinous sins against nature. That was especially true now that it was confirmed that he was teaching someone else everything that he knew; spreading all of that volatile witchcraft was something that could not be allowed to continue because it was impossible to know what that new person would do with their knowledge. Jean seemed like a decent enough person, but he was walking a very slippery slope.

The problem was that Cedric really should never have spared Jean to begin with, but now that he had, he needed to figure out what he was going to do with him. He had been very helpful during this whole assignment but would that be all? Would it be right to just let him be and go about his own life now? It didn't seem right to just turn a blind eye toward him now, especially now that he had taken an apprentice and clearly had no intention of stopping his study of magic anytime in the near future. No, Jean-Luc

Gerard would continue to be a danger, no matter how good his intentions were.

Cedric did not want to kill him. He had already tried to but couldn't bring himself to do it, and that fact had not changed. There had to be something else, another way to solve the conundrum without resorting to running Jean through with his blade. Even now, recognizing the threat that he still posed was not enough to make him want to execute him.

There needed to be another way to neutralize him and prevent all of that knowledge he knew from spreading or at least be put to better use. That was when a thought occurred to him that seemed to set off a light bulb in his brain, a notion that was a gamble but might work out well for the Knights Templar.

Just as his thoughts started to click into place, his phone rang. It was Edmund, with as good of timing as ever. He was probably checking in on him unnecessarily like he did before, no doubt. It was certainly not a social call.

Cedric grudgingly answered. "Aye?"

"We would like an update on your progress." It was just as Cedric predicted it would be. There was no small talk or pleasantries from him, just a cold analytical question. It was like talking to a computer.

"I was going to be calling you soon enough with a full report, but if you really must know now, then it is like this... The Dracule Bloodline were killing people and taking their blood in order to rejuvenate the remains of Vlad the Impaler. As it were, he was actually a vampire. A real one. And he slaughtered his own cult and then tried to kill me. But don't you fret, Edmund, because I handled it."

There was silence on the other end of the phone for a long moment. None of those things were probably exactly what he thought he was going to hear from Cedric. It was a much stranger update than most of the reports the Templar received from their knights.

"He was a vampire, you say? An actual vampire?" Edmund sounded like he was on the verge of breaking into a fit of laughter.

"Aye, he was very real. I saw his fangs and everything. He ran on the ceiling of the cave."

"Did he turn into a little bat too?" Edmund asked smugly, obviously not taking the report very seriously.

"I can't say that he did, no. But I didn't give him much of a chance. I was too busy saving the world." Cedric left out the part of the story involving getting help from a user of witchcraft and his apprentice. That omission was probably for the best. "You probably wouldn't understand."

"Let's say that you really did stop some vampire. What did you mean by it being handled?"

"Simple, I lured him out into the outdoors on a beautiful sunny morning. Watched him cook right in front of me until there was nothing left."

There was silence on the other end of the phone again.

"I expect that some of what you are saying is simply hyperbolic." Edmund certainly did not sound entirely convinced by what was absolutely the truth. "The rest is just drivel."

"You're wrong."

"Whatever the case...whether there is any truth to this story of yours...we expect some kind of result from this venture of yours. The Templar have grown rather tired of you giving us absolutely nothing. First, you galivant around that ghost house in America with nothing to show for it except for Arthur's corpse, the body of one of our best. And now, you spend all of this time investigating the Dracule cult, and all you have are outlandish stories about vampires and nothing else?"

Hearing the statistics spelled out like that definitely stung a little. It was hard to deny that Cedric's brief tenure as a knight of Templar had been anything but a failure. He needed a win, and he needed one soon. Edmund was not just saying all of this to upset Cedric; he was voicing what was no doubt the collective frustration of the rest of the Templar too.

"Listen to me and do it very, very carefully, Cedric. You hang on to every word that I am about to say. Consider every syllable. You need to show us that you are worth keeping around. Prove to us that you belong among the honored ranks of the Knights Templar because so far, you have not exactly done that, have you? If you can't do that, then we will have no choice but to take that sword away from you. That blade is a privilege to wield. Never forget that."

The phone clicked, and Edmund had abruptly hung up without a proper goodbye.

Cedric stood there in silence for a long moment. Everything that he had worked so hard for was slipping away. Even the victories were stained by how they were being perceived. Helping to slay an actual vampire was ignored because it was not what the Knights Templar were really searching for, not unless they had concrete evidence to back it up.

Cedric was still so new to their ranks and still needed to prove himself. Every action he took should reflect his desire to keep improving his station and to assist the Knights Templar. But he had already gone behind their backs numerous times or disobeyed orders believing that he knew better. He was putting everything at risk because of his own hubris.

That needed to stop. He needed to do his job and to do it well and properly. There was only one real way to do that and to reaffirm his loyalty to the Knights Templar. He needed to correct the mistakes he had already made. He needed to make amends for it and set things back on the right track. There was really only one way to do that.

Cedric knew exactly what he needed to do—even if he did not want to do it. He needed to go through with what he should have done from the very beginning. He needed to bring down Jean-Luc Gerard.

16

PROBLEMS AT HOME

It was nice to be back home in his shop. Usually, it would be a moment when he would take it easy and sit in silence for a while, letting everything that happened wash over him. Sometimes he would pick up one of the books on the shelves and just flip through it to relax. It should be a time of solitude and reflection—but that was impossible with Thaddeus Rose with him. Calm was not exactly an option with Thaddeus around.

"Look, I don't want to be the one that said that I told you so, but I told you so! That was a real vampire down there! A real one!" Thaddeus had been raving about Vlad the Impaler's remains the entire trip home, and he didn't seem like he was going to stop anytime soon. He was especially proud that he had been the one to keep saying that it could be actual vampires and had been kept being—understandably—brushed off for even making that kind of suggestion. In the end, he had been right about the vampires, and he was not going to let anyone hear the end of it. Jean half expected him to go running out into the streets of New Orleans and tell the whole world about how right he was. "I wish Kaleb had been there with his camera! That would have been something amazing for us! Proof that I had been the one to find a real vampire and even slay one too!"

It was very typical of Thad to completely take credit for finding the vampire when in actuality, it was really the Dracule Bloodline that had been the ones to discover the location of Vlad the Impaler's body and had also been the ones to revive him with all of that blood. As far as slaying Vlad too, that was definitely more of a group effort that Thad was letting on. He didn't seem to recognize the contributions of others, or if he did, he did not mind completely taking credit away from them. Jean wasn't surprised by that point by Thaddeus Rose's ego. That was just who he was.

"Like think about it this way. *Dracula* was at least inspired by Vlad the Impaler, or maybe even Bram Stoker knew the truth about him, meaning that Vlad essentially was the famous vampire. When you look at it that way, the way that it actually was, isn't it pretty clear that we just defeated Dracula himself? Can you believe that? One of the most famous names in the world, and *we* stopped him! We stopped Dracula!" Thad laughed giddily, in disbelief of what they had just done. When he put it like that, it did seem absolutely crazy.

Dracula was not supposed to be real, but he was—at least kind of.

Jean, as an instructor and mentor, could not let his student revel in his cockiness. He had to knock him down a peg and bring him back to at least some kind of reality. That might not have been what Thaddeus wanted, but that was what he needed. Feeling accomplished was great, but getting completely absorbed by that victory was not good and would probably lead to defeat in the end. Pride was dangerous even at times when it felt like you had every right to take pride in yourself.

"We could have done better," Jean said.

Thad looked baffled, like he had been slapped in the face. "What do you mean we could have done better? How could we have possibly done better than that? We did everything right! I just said we slayed Dracula himself, and we did! It does not get much better than that!"

"Yes, it does," Jean said firmly. "We could have used our magic more effectively, and by that, I mean that you could have used your magic at all. But I don't blame you too much for it. You are still new and still learning. I did not expect you to get it down overnight, but I hoped that in a life or death situation, you might be able to manifest something. Sometimes that's when your connection with magic is at its strongest, when there is no choice but to use it or lose your life. That isn't what happened, though."

Thad's enthusiasm diminished and fell to a more reasonable level, taking some of that cockiness away just like Jean wanted. "I know, but I will keep studying it. I don't want that to happen again next time. If we are ever in a situation like that again, I want to be able to get out of it, or at least defend myself better. I want to be able to use witchcraft."

It was nice to hear his dedication be reaffirmed. There were times when Thaddeus felt like an ungrateful teenager in school, refusing to actually do any of the work while still expecting to get a perfect score on his report card. But then there were the brief moments—like when Thad first asked to become his student—when a more genuine and vulnerable side of Thaddeus Rose managed to break through his facade of self-assurance.

"You will if you keep studying like you are. I will make sure that you will be able to tap into the real magic of the world if you keep putting in the time and the effort. Let's just look at that whole excursion to Transylvania as a field trip but now, here in this library, is where we need to get back to the real work, where the real learning can take place. Sometimes it's good to get your hands dirty, but a lot of time, when it comes to learning about witchcraft, you just need to get the information in those pages into your brain however you can."

Thaddeus understood. "That sounds great, but I don't think I am alert enough to be able to read more tonight. I'm exhausted."

"That's totally fine." Jean could not sleight him for being exhausted since Jean was absolutely exhausted too. It was amazing how a venture like that could just drain all of the energy out of a body, but at least all of their blood was not drained. Fighting a crazy cult and running away from an actual vampire were very tiring things to do in the long run, and Jean was going to need probably a few days' worth of sleep before he would feel refreshed after that. Luckily, he had no plans of doing anything like that again anytime soon. He was just going to enjoy being back home and focus on his teachings again. "Go home, get some rest. Take the next few days off, and then we will pick our lessons back up once we both have gotten some sleep."

"That sounds good to me," Thad said. "You have a good couple of days then, Jean."

"You too."

Thaddeus gave him a tired wave before leaving the store. Jean locked the door behind him to make sure no late-night customers or drunken wanderers from Bourbon Street decided to try to come in. The store would be closed for the next few days while he rested and wouldn't reopen until he was ready to take on the world again.

The skull of Vlad the Impaler stared back at him with those hollow sockets of darkness. Not long ago, and only briefly, there had been actual eyes there—eyes that had glared at Jean with so much want and with so much hunger. The mind behind those had been voracious, focused, and never would have stopped going after what it wanted once it saw it. Now, thankfully, those eyes were gone, and the vision of endless bloodlust was gone with them.

That monstrous face was gone, the flesh burned away by the sunlight, but those fangs remained, still sharp and still probably more than capable of tearing into someone's throat. It was so strange to think how only days ago, that skull was brimming with newfound life, but that was gone now, and Jean couldn't have been more relieved about that.

The world didn't need an ancient vampire in it or his crazy cult of worshipers.

The skull of Vlad the Impaler would go where the rest of Jean's dangerous items were stored—the locked closet in the back of the bookshop. Unlike most closets, it was warded with all kinds of runes and symbols to keep people from getting into it, but more importantly, to keep the things inside of it from ever getting out. The majority of the things kept in that closet were spell books and old grimoires that had actual power inside of them and contained all kinds of knowledge that could be incredibly dangerous to the outside world. The skull might not have had pages of powerful incantations, but it still was easily one of the most dangerous things that would be in that closet.

Jean was going to make sure that he kept blood far away from that skull. He would never take it out of that closet, and he would make sure not even a single drop of blood would ever touch the bone of that skull.

"It's strange to have survived something like that, eh?"

Jean turned to find Cedric McKellan standing in the back of the store behind the cash register. He leaned against the counter, his gleaming sword dangling from his hand, making sure that it could be seen. Despite how casually he was standing, there was a clear intended threat to Cedric's presence. He was trying to frighten Jean; otherwise, he would have just taken the front door like a normal person and not have sneaked around to go unnoticed that whole time.

Jean stayed calm, doing his best to ignore the blade that was already drawn. "I am sorry, but we are closed. You can come back in a few days, and I will be happy to help you with whatever you need."

"Oh, you already did," Cedric said and tapped his sword on the stack of books beside him. It was the few books that had information on vampires that Jean had given him at the beginning of all of this. "Those books came in handy, but it was the firsthand experience that was really impressive. You can learn a lot from it..."

Besides the obvious threat of the drawn sword, the young British man seemed different than he had throughout the entirety of their time together in Romania. He usually seemed so conflicted but always leaned on the calm side, but there was a tension now that wasn't there before. Whatever the case, this surprise visit was not exactly welcome and was not something that Jean was enjoying very much.

"So, can I help you find any other books then? Because again, we are closed, and you will have to come back when the store is open."

Cedric did not move a muscle. He stayed exactly where he was, and it creeped Jean out. Every instinct in his body told him to run away because deep down, he had a feeling that he knew what this visit was. This was what he had feared that whole time, had believed was always the reason that Cedric McKellan had come back into his life so soon—the Templar knight was there to finish the job.

"Your knowledge on the more peculiar things in this world

is incredible, Jean, but it is also undeniably dangerous. You know things that mortals should not know, that we should not even ponder. There are powers in the world that should never be wielded, but you wield them anyway."

"We've been over this," Jean said through gritted teeth, his anger rising. "I use witchcraft sparingly and only ever to try to help people. That is all."

Cedric gave a solemn nod followed by a tired sigh. "I hoped that that reason would be enough. I truly did. I believe you have good intentions yourself. But that doesn't matter. It doesn't matter what your intentions are when it comes to that experience, silly, because you are not the only one using witchcraft. There can't be exceptions. Especially because now I see that you are sharing your sinful knowledge with others, teaching people like Thaddeus Rose. I don't know him very well but well enough to know that a narcissist should not have power like that. You know that too, obviously, and you are still helping him anyway. What do you think will happen when a person like that knows how to perform spells and actual witchcraft? Nothing good. I doubt he would have the restraint that you have shown. I really doubt it."

"He's not my ideal student either, but I think you're being a bit paranoid. Personally, I think showing him how to do a little bit of magic will be good for him in the long run. I think it's far more likely that he will get something good out of it than him becoming some kind of big apocalyptic supernatural threat. Trust me, he's not competent enough at anything to actually be any kind of problem in the future."

"That's a chance that we cannot take, Jean." Cedric took a step forward. "If we keep allowing things to slide or leave them unchecked, then the problem will just grow and fester until eventually, it reaches a breaking point by which point, it could be impossible to control or contain."

"You people should not be trying to control anything!" Jean shouted out, alarmed by his own anger. The Knights Templar and their crusade against witchcraft disgusted him, though, so it was hard to restrain himself when it came to that topic. "It has nothing to do with you outside of you all inserting yourself where you don't belong, trying to make decisions about things that none of you even bother to try to understand! I hoped you were different than the rest but look at you now, Cedric. You are just more of the same. Really disappointing, but it is what it is. You have clearly made your bed, and now you have got to sleep in it, man."

Jean took a step back and held out his arms.

"So, come on then, you want to finish what you started at the Winchester Mystery House? Then get on with it! Give it your best shot."

Cedric seemed a little uncertain about how to proceed, but he took a step forward anyway. "I, too, hoped that you would be different. It seems that we have both disappointed each other. I would appreciate it if you don't intend to resist."

Jean laughed and said, "Don't be so stupid. Of course, I intend to resist."

With that, Jean-Luc Gerard went into survival mode. He

didn't usually use witchcraft as a direct weapon or to defend himself, but now he really had no choice. He would do whatever he had to do to not let Cedric end him. He was not going to give him and the Knights Templar the satisfaction. If he was going to die, he was going to go down swinging and hopefully leave a few scars behind in his wake.

Jean mouthed a levitation spell. It was a rather simple spell that he learned early on in his studies of magic, but it was very versatile as well and could work in very different ways depending on the situation. In this instance, he focused on whatever was around him and realized that the library of books in his store could actually be an arsenal of their own, ammunition for him to use against his assailant.

Cedric took a few steps forward, and Jean held out his hands, chanting the spell. When he did, a few books flew off of their shelves and hit Cedric. The Templar was startled by the sudden attack as the first couple of books hit his upper body. As a couple more launched through the air, he tried to swipe them out of the way with his sword; he managed to knock away a couple but not all of the projectiles. Jean spoke faster and put more energy into it, increasing the power of the spell itself. More and more books propelled off of the shelves and counters at once, sending waves of hardcovers at Cedric. He did his best to knock them away, but many got through. Some of those books were hefty and thick and were almost like cannonballs when they made contact with him. The Templar knight got knocked down a couple of times but still kept getting back up, trying to push through the maelstrom of literature. He wanted to get rid of witchcraft, but Jean intended on burying him in it. He would do everything he could to make sure that all of that collected forbidden knowledge that the Knights Templar were so worried about would be their downfall.

Cedric wasn't going down easy, though. Books kept smacking him in the head or hitting him in the ribs, or slamming his limbs, but none of it completely stopped his advance. He kept walking across the store, and as he drew nearer, there were fewer and fewer books for Jean to throw at him with magic. Cedric was determined and refused to let himself be knocked out by any of the levitating projectiles.

Jean backed away slowly toward the front door, starting to lose ground. Book after book rocketed at his enemy, but it wasn't enough. He was relentless, and Jean's strength was being sapped with each word he spoke. That was the kind of thing that many people did not realize about magic. It was not simple or easy to perform. It was incredibly taxing on the one performing it; it exhausted every fiber of your being, including the mind, the body, and the soul. Jean was starting to struggle to maintain his defense, and he would not be able to keep it up for much longer.

Cedric got close, and Jean was practically shouting the spell now, trying so hard to keep his enemy away. Cedric threw out his arm, but instead of a sword coming at Jean as he had expected, it was a syringe instead. The needle went straight into Jean's neck, and he, still chanting, stepped away in surprise. All of the books that were levitating plopped to the floor and settled as Jean put a hand to his neck where he had been injected. That was not the kind of puncture wound that he was expecting; he figured that it would be a much larger one in his chest, but that gleaming sword was free of any blood.

"What...what did you just do?" Jean asked weakly. He felt like he was about to pass out but was not entirely sure if it was from the strange injection or from the magic he had just expended. "What is that?"

"Oh, this?" Cedric pulled out the empty syringe. "This will just help you relax, put you to sleep for a bit. Can't have you using more of that magic and making a mess. Just look at this place. I would hate to be the one that has to clean that up."

Jean could feel the world around him starting to tilt, and his body start to push him toward unconsciousness. He didn't want to pass out, though, not before he got answers. His leg crumbled to one knee, and he stared at the lowered sword in Cedric's hand.

"Why didn't you just...why didn't you just kill me? I thought...I thought that's what you were going to...going to do."

"Luckily for you, I am not here to end your life. As much as I'm sure that my superiors want that, I am going to convince them that you are far more valuable alive than you would be dead."

Jean wasn't exactly sure what he meant by that, and his fading consciousness was not making it any easier to figure it out either. He could see his store in shambles, with his collection of books scattered all about. It hurt to know that his safe haven had been defiled and that he could not stop his enemy. But why had he been allowed to live? It didn't make sense.

Everything started to grow dark, and he felt like he was back in that cavern deep beneath the earth again. This was somehow even darker—and he didn't know when he would ever see the light again.

17

A TOOL FOR THE TEMPLAR

When consciousness found Jean again, he was in a place that he did not recognize. He was laying on a cold stone floor. He knew that much without even opening his eyes. His body recovered slowly from whatever it was that he had been injected with by Cedric. He was furious that Cedric had even been able to do that to him but still wondered why it had not been the top of his sword that pierced him instead. There had to be a good reason that Cedric had kept him alive and took him somewhere instead of just finishing things right then and there. There had to be a piece that Jean was missing.

It took quite a bit of strength just to open his eyes, but he finally managed. When he did, he could see that he was laying in an old chamber, like something in a castle. There were stone walls with large sprawling tapestries stretched across them and an enormous fireplace on the other side of the room where a small fire was burning.

"Aw, you're awake. Good." Cedric appeared on one side of the chamber.

"What the hell did you do?" Jean asked, trying to find the strength to even speak. "Where are we?"

"This right here is one of the Knights Templar's many fortresses that are scared about the world."

Jean was getting tired of being knocked out, abducted by people, and lugged to their top-secret hideout. First, the Dracules had done that to him back in Romania, and now Cedric had done the same. He had escaped from one crazy cult only to end up as a prisoner for another. There was apparently just no way to win.

Cedric crouched so that they were closer as Jean tried to sit up. Jean cracked his neck and rolled his eyes. "You couldn't have at least put me in a bed or something?"

"No," Cedric said. "You are currently our prisoner, but there could be a way to make accommodations like that possible. I just need to talk to a few people about it first. When it comes down to it, though, Jean, would you be willing to help us? You apparently love teaching your knowledge to others, so teach us, give us what we need to improve our crusade."

Jean managed a thin smile and chuckled. "Oh, I see. You took me because you guys are tired of losing and need something to give you an edge? You want to pump me for information and then slit my throat just like you've done to all of the others. You're not offering for my assistance, you are demanding I help you. Well, I hate to break it to you, but there is no way in hell that that is ever going to happen. I don't turn on my own."

Cedric frowned. "I had an inkling that that was what you were going to say. That is quite alright. You can either cooperate, or the Templar have other ways of making you give us what we want. It's as I said, it is still not even decided if you helping us will be allowed."

"It doesn't matter if it's allowed or whatever because it is not happening either way. There is no universe where I let you people use me for what I know."

"How is it any different than you giving me some of the books from your shop? You were willing to give me information then. This doesn't have to be any different."

"That was back when I still thought that you had a mind of your own and a spine. That was back when I hoped that you weren't like the rest of these people, buying into all of their crap. I was wrong about that. If I had known that you were this far gone, I never would have helped you with any of that. None of it."

Cedric looked strangely hurt by that. "Either way, willingly or not, I know that you would be a great asset to our efforts. You kept talking about the Templar not understanding witchcraft or magic...now you can give us a chance to understand it. You can be the one that helps us learn all about it. All you need to do is show us what you know, just like you were doing with that buffoon Thaddeus Rose."

"Thaddeus is not perfect. Hell, he is kind of the worst, but I would much rather he know all of those things than all of you people. He's just ignorant of the truth. You all willingly ignore it and try to destroy it. If you had the chance, you and your buddies would probably burn down my whole shop and everything inside of it, wouldn't you!?"

Cedric didn't say anything, and a bolt of fear ran up Jean's spine. He hoped that they had not burned his store to the ground, but before he could even ask, someone else entered the room.

It was a man, older than Cedric, wearing a very expensive suit. His brown hair was neatly parted to the side of his head; he looked well-groomed. He had an immediate air of aristocracy about him, as if he had been born to inherit all of the power in the world. He had a ruby-red ring on one of the fingers of his right hand, which matched Cedric's own, a symbol of the Templar probably, and he no doubt had a matching shortsword sheathed in his suit jacket too.

As he entered, Cedric immediately seemed to fall in line and make way for him. It was clear that he was someone that was more highly ranked within the Templar. He certainly carried himself that way.

"Aw, so this is the elusive Jean-Luc, is it?"

"That's me," Jean said, groggily standing up straight. "Am I supposed to know who you are?"

The man gave a little laugh. "No. I would not be very good at my job if you did. My name is Tristan Malloy. I am the current grandmaster of the Order of the Knights Templar."

"You're the big boss, huh? The manager? Good because I

would love to file a complaint against several of your employees. They have been nothing but a pain in my ass for a while now. They are constantly stalking me. They are constantly harassing me. And if I am being completely honest, sir, your employees have tried to kill me quite a few times. It's far from the best customer service I have ever seen."

The well-dressed man did not seem impressed. He barely seemed to even pay Jean any mind at all. He didn't care what he had to say. He looked down at his captive with mild interest, but it was as if he was inspecting a car instead of a person, like he was trying to judge how fast the car could go just from getting a first impression of it.

Tristan turned his attention to Cedric and pointed at Jean. He had a shining red ring that matched Cedric's own. "This is the one then? The occult expert you told me about?"

"He is," Cedric said. "This is Jean-Luc Gerard. He is not only well versed in all kinds of aspects of the occult, but he is also a practitioner of witchcraft and magic. I have seen him do it numerous times with my own eyes. The things he can do...it's really quite remarkable."

"And you are still determined to follow through with what you brought to my attention?"

"I am," Cedric said.

Jean would have loved to have known what they were talking about, but unfortunately, he was not a mind reader. He just had to wait and figure it out once it was actually verbally presented to him.

"Brilliant..." Tristan looked very pleased and glanced back at Jean with the utmost arrogance. "The Knights Templar needs someone with intimate knowledge of the forbidden that is willing to stain their soul. Someone that is willing to do the kinds of things that we are not willing to do."

"That's right, I forgot," Jean said, spitting on the floor. "You are not willing to even get close to magic, but you are willing to take a person's head off with a sword...how noble of you to have such high moral standards, man."

"We are willing to destroy evil, yes. You may see it as savagery, but it is simply necessity. We will protect this world from those that unleash the unnatural like yourself."

"But now you realize how helpful it would be to have me on your side," Jean said, nodding his head as the pieces all came together. "Makes sense since it's obvious you guys don't know much of anything about witchcraft except that you don't like it."

Jean peered at Cedric, who had become very quiet since his superior came into the room and took charge of the conversation.

"But let me make this real simple for you. I don't care what your offer is. My answer is no, and it is always going to be no, whether it is today, tomorrow, or any other day in the future. That is not going to change. That no will always be the same answer time and time again."

Tristan smirked, unconvinced. "I know you say that now but human beings are such fickle creatures. Minds go back and forth so very often, and your mind will change one way or another."

That didn't sound good, but Jean didn't expect it to be. All of their cryptic threats did not change anything for him, though.

"You said that our guest here owns a bookshop full of all manner of artifacts and cursed objects? Spell books and other such items?"

"That's right, sir," Cedric said. "Right in the heart of the French Quarter. It is a stockpile of years of work amassing information on the topic. Some of the things in there, I am sure, have real power that could be a threat to the people outside of that bookshop. And Jean here is tame. If all of that fell into the wrong hands, then we could really have a problem on our hands."

"That sounds quite unsafe, don't you think?" Tristan asked Jean. "It may be for the best that we put a match or two to all of those spell books of yours and burn it to the ground. I am sure witches' grimoires burn just as well as regular books do. If their owners were any indication, then those books would probably burn as brightly as the witches that the Templar has put to the stake."

The aristocratic aura remained, but every word was laced with such vile hostility, and Jean could tell that Tristan Malloy was the kind of man that would follow through with his threats. He really was trying to strongarm Jean into agreeing to help them. Jean didn't want to, and he couldn't think of anything worse, but if it meant salvaging his bookstore, then maybe he would have to give in—or at least look like he was giving in. He wanted to stick to his own personal codes and continue to refuse, but he really couldn't any longer. At the very least, it would give him time to maybe figure out a way to escape or to stop the Knights Templar.

"Alright, man. Alright. I hear you." Jean prepared himself for the words that he was about to let come out of his mouth, words that he hated even thinking about, let alone actually saying aloud. "I will help you with what you need."

Both Tristan and especially Cedric looked shocked that he was accepting their offer to form an alliance. Neither of them must have thought that he would ever give in to their pressure, and Jean didn't think that he would either. But, as the expression always went, desperate times called for desperate measures. He just needed to do whatever he could to survive. He knew that if he continued not to comply, he would end up like all of the other magic users that the Knights Templar had come across. They would execute him and then probably still burn his bookstore to the ground anyway.

"Happy?" Jean asked.

Tristan smiled. "We are elated."

Behind Tristan, he saw a flash of guilt cross the young Cedric's face, but it was too late for apologies or regrets. Despite working together twice now, Cedric McKellan had proven to Jean that he was not a friend. He was one of his most dangerous foes.

Jean would help the Knights Templar as long as he needed to—but he would make sure that it was the least helpful assistance that he could possibly offer. It wasn't all bad, though. There was a possibility that this could allow him to get into a position to completely tear the Knights Templar apart from the inside out. That would be great.

"So... tell us some secrets about magic."

EPILOGUE

THE RUINED LIBRARY

Thaddeus actually felt very good and had gotten plenty of rest in the few days since they had gotten back to New Orleans. He felt rejuvenated and ready to dive back into whatever magical lessons Jean had planned for him.

The music of New Orleans was something that he usually barely even noticed, but today, every beat and rhythm moved through his body, and he couldn't help but dance a little. There was nothing quite like surviving a fight with a vampiric cult to brighten one's mood, apparently. He just felt so happy to be alive and basked in the sun—like a vampire never could—as he walked down the street. He knew those sidewalks of the French Quarter so well now, having performed on many of them to the delight of many. When you performed magic on the streets and curbsides, the entire city became your stage. He reveled in having such a large potential audience—and really wanted to always impress them.

That was really why he wanted to be able to use authentic kinds of magic. He just wanted to show people something that they had truly never seen before. That was always his goal, but the usual magic tricks of deception and illusion had their own limitations. Jean would continue to teach him things that he could use to really surprise people, and he could not wait to see what he could come up with when he had magic in his hands.

Thad reached the front door of Jean's occult ship and tried to pull it open, but it didn't budge. Usually, he did not have to pay attention and just walked in. It was usually open at that hour, but apparently, now it was not. The closed sign still hung, but the hours on it showed that Jean should have been there. Maybe he had taken a sick day. They had been through quite a lot in recent days, so he could not exactly blame him for not coming back to work yet.

That was okay—since Thaddeus had been given a spare key to the store. Jean had told him that the key was supposed to be used sparingly but this seemed like a good time to use it. Thad could get inside and start going through some of the books on his own. Even without his tutor, he could take the initiative and still try to learn. Besides, Jean was probably just going to have him read if he was there anyway, and he could do that on his own.

Although, Thaddeus hoped that now that they had gone through all of that together, Jean would finally show him some of the exciting stuff that Thad could do with his own hands. He was tired of just reading about hypotheticals on the page.

Thad put his key in and turned it. He could feel the latch

move, and then he opened the door. He expected to find the usual sight of a vast trove of supernatural knowledge waiting on the shelves—but hardly anything was on the shelves.

The whole store looked like it had been trashed and torn apart. Books lay all over the place in various states of disarray like someone had gone through and tossed each and every one off of the shelves where they had been stored. It almost looked like someone had broken in and robbed the place, but instead of just taking everything, they were looking for something in particular and moved everything out of the way. Then again, it also looked like the aftermath of some earthquake or something that had knocked everything out of place. It was an absolute mess.

"Jean!?" Thad called out. "Jean, are you here!?"

There was no response. Thaddeus picked up a book and looked around, hoping for any kind of sign of what the hell had happened there, but there was nothing specific that he could see, just the piles of books lying around in heaps. One thing he knew about Jean was that he was very particular about the storage of the books he had in the shop. He would never have left the store in that kind of state. Maybe he hadn't seen it yet, or maybe he hadn't had a choice at all.

Thaddeus stood there for a long moment, among the ruins of that store and the messy remains of what had once been such an impressive library. He wanted to clean it all up, and he planned to, but first, he needed to know what had happened and, in particular, what had happened to Jean.

There was only one person that would probably know what happened or where to find him. Thad dropped the book he was examining back into the messy pile on the floor and sprinted out of the shop. He made sure to lock the front door and then turned around to find a woman waiting to go inside. Thad stood in front of the door, trying not to make it obvious that he was trying to conceal what might be able to be seen inside.

"Hi, I was just hoping to check out some of the books in there. People keep telling me that this is the best place to go if you need something authentic."

"It definitely is the best place, yes," Thad said. "Everything inside is kept to the highest standard, and the store only stocks actual helpful information."

She smiled, but then that went away when she saw the closed sign.

"Are you open?"

Thad tried to think quickly on his feet. "Unfortunately, not today. The store is in the middle of renovations. Yes. Some very serious renovations. I am not sure how long it will take, but hopefully it'll be open soon."

It all hinged on if he could find Jean or at least figure out what happened to him. The customer seemed understanding and left, leaving Thad to go try to carry out his plan. Once it seemed like he didn't look strange, he broke into a run through the city and didn't dare stop until he reached the house of Mama May.

There was a line of people looking to meet with her, but

he pushed through them, much to their collected chagrin and the complete disdain on their faces when they saw him pushing his way to the front of the line. He didn't care if they liked it or not. The safety of Jean far outweighed whatever issues they were having. A disappearance and a defaced bookstore were far more important than who that guy was going to marry or what grade that girl would get on her upcoming test. Those issues were trivial in comparison to what he was going through at that moment.

"You're cutting the line!"

"You need to go to the back!"

"We got here first!"

"Excuse you, asshole!"

Thad pushed his way to the front in spite of their anger toward him. They would just have to get over it. All of those visitors looked shocked when he threw the front door open and stormed into the house.

"Mama May! Mama May!"

Thaddeus stomped into the living room, where the old fortune-teller sat across from her current visitor, holding her bleeding hand and offering her a premonition of the days to come. The old woman snapped out of her trance at the sound of his interruption and turned in Thad's direction.

"How dare you barge into my home!?"

Thaddeus stormed in anyway, probably looking like an

absolute madman. He didn't care how he looked. That wasn't important.

Mama May rose from her chair furiously, her legs trembling. Still, despite her physical stature, he could feel the power radiating from her and knew that his trespassing was not appreciated, but he had to do it. He stomped up to her, breathing heavily.

"I'm sorry, alright!? But this is important!" He glanced at the young woman sitting in the chair that had had her future read. "Actually important." He turned back to Mama May. "Jean is gone."

The old woman processed what he said, and her wrinkled face grew very grave. She turned to the young woman in the chair. "I am sorry, my dear, but we are going to have to pick this up another time."

"Really?" the woman asked, looking incredibly offended. She glared at Thad, probably wondering why him barging in was even allowed.

"I am afraid so," Mama May said sweetly. "Come back tomorrow, and we will get back to it. Free of charge, of course."

The customer seemed somewhat appeased but shot Thad another leer before leaving.

Mama May turned her attention back to Thaddeus. He could see the worry in her eyes.

"What do you mean by gone?"

"I was hoping you could tell me," Thad said. He was not the

psychic, after all. "Because his store has been completely trashed like a bomb went off in there. He's not answering his phone."

Mama May looked even more sullen. "Then it did come to pass. It is just as I warned him."

"What do you mean?" Thaddeus remembered being there for that premonition but did not remember the specifics. He had been too busy reeling from his own prediction to worry much about what she had said to Jean. He just needed a reminder. "The part where you said that he and I would drown in blood together?"

"No, no, that future seems to have been avoided. No, I told him that he would be faced with two separate entities that meant to harm him and that if one did not succeed, then the other might. It seems that is most likely the case."

Thad's brain was racing frantically as he considered everything that she was saying. "So, we beat the Dracules and Vlad the Impaler and all of those people but the other entity...the Templar...?"

Mama May gave a grave nod, so still that it was barely even noticeable as a confirmation.

"Cedric. Cedric did something just like you told Jean that he would. His doom or whatever..."

Mama May nodded again. "Some futures can be avoided. Some cannot be so easily missed. Jean-Luc Gerard has been taken by the ones that hate our kind, that magic."

The Knights Templar had abducted him. After everything that they went through with Cedric at their sides, Thad

had hoped that any of that animosity was gone or at least that there was some kind of understanding, but apparently there wasn't. All of their worries about Cedric that they had from the beginning were apparently warranted in the end. As validating as that was, he wished that it wasn't the case. It wasn't satisfying being right when it meant losing his mentor.

"So, what do we do?" Thaddeus asked.

"Take a deep breath, child, and prepare for whatever the future may bring."

Mama May held his hand.

"Come. Let us see what you might need to be ready to face."

There was a time when Thaddeus Rose would never have spoken to a fortune-teller, but now, he wanted nothing more than to hear what she had to say.

Thad took her hand, hoping that there was good news about the days ahead.

THE END

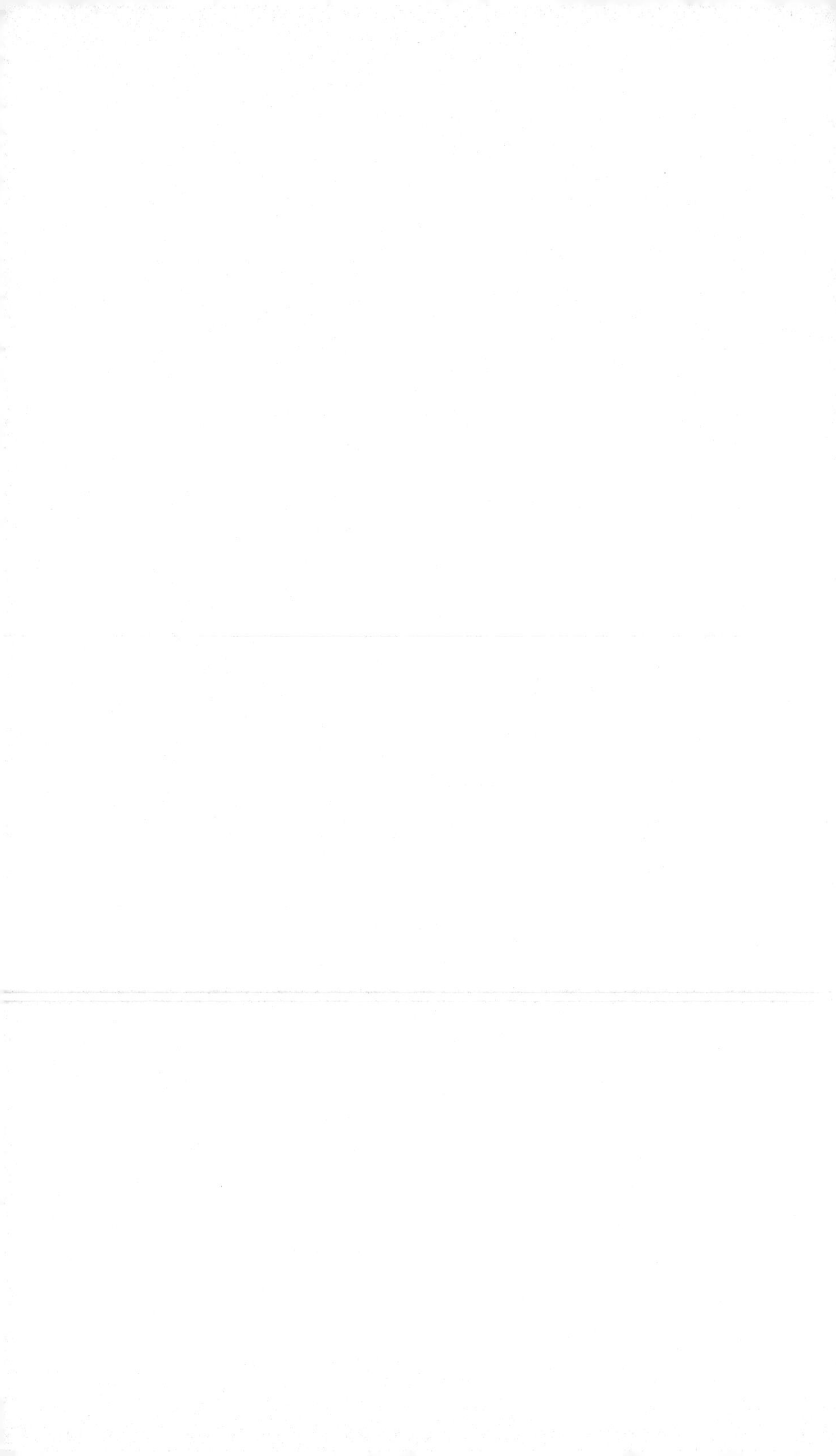

Printed in Great Britain
by Amazon

21541127R00150